NIGHT OVER
THE SOLOMONS

NIGHT OVER THE SOLOMONS

LOUIS L'AMOUR

BANTAM BOOKS

TORONTO • NEW YORK • LONDON • SYDNEY • AUCKLAND

NIGHT OVER THE SOLOMONS

A Bantam Book / published by arrangement with the author

The Louis L'Amour Collection / October 1986

If you would be interested in receiving bookends for The Louis L'Amour Collection, please write to this address for information:

The Louis L'Amour Collection
Bantam Books
P.O. Box 956
Hicksville, New York 11802

ISBN 0-553-06307-3

Published simultaneously in the United States and Canada

Bantam Books are published by Bantam Books, Inc. Its trademark, consisting of the words "Bantam Books" and the portrayal of a rooster, is Registered in U.S. Patent and Trademark Office and in other countries. Marca Registrada. Bantam Books, Inc., 666 Fifth Avenue, New York, New York 10103.

PRINTED IN THE UNITED STATES OF AMERICA

0 9 8 7 6 5 4 3 2 1

To the memory of all those soldiers,
sailors, and pilots of fortune from whom
I learned so much during my knockabout days.

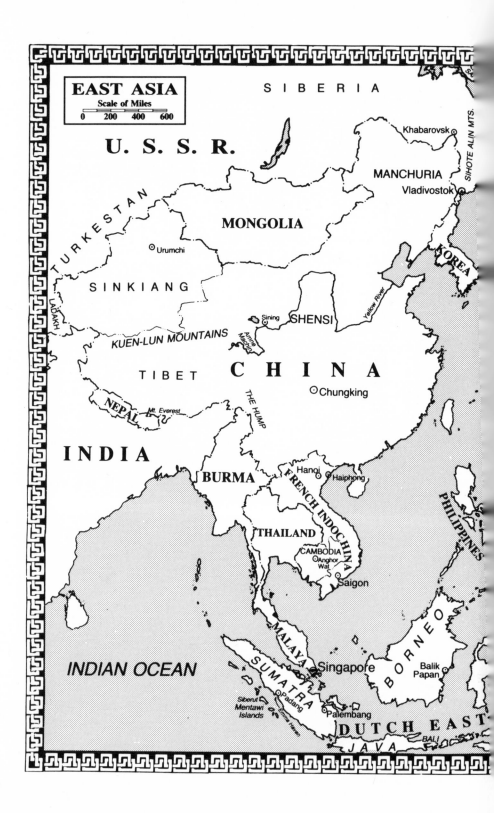

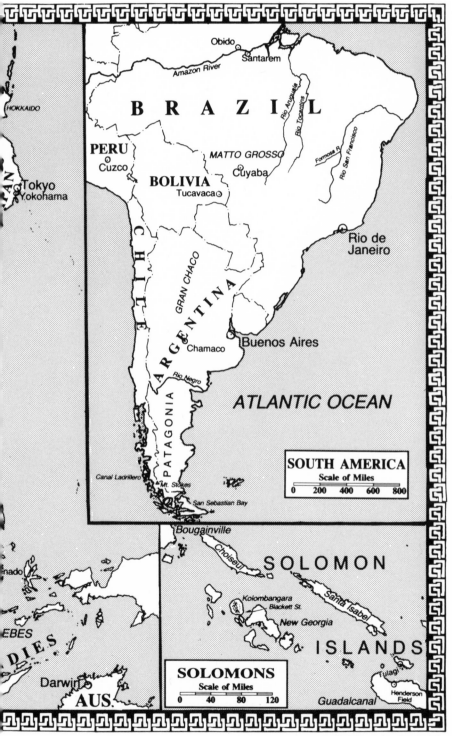

Map by Alan McKnight

FOREWORD

There have been, in every period of civilization, those men (and some women) who have lived on the outer fringes. They were frequent on our own frontiers as well as in Australia, the Pacific islands, Africa, Canada, Latin America, and wherever else men faced the unknown with the chance of wealth or fame for the survivors. The men of whom I write in the stories in this collection were such adventurers.

Back in my pre–World War II knockabout days, I got to know a lot of men like my heroes Turk Madden, Mike Thorne, and Steve Cowan. Some were exploring the jungle for gold, diamonds, or orchids. Others sought their fortune fishing for pearls, prospecting for oil, or flying planes for Chinese warlords. Many of them had a boss, but some were loners operating on a shoestring out in the great beyond.

My Turk Madden stories grew out of an unrealized dream I shared with one of the latter fortune seekers. I'd become friendly with a bush pilot who would land a seaplane on a wet handkerchief if the price was right. He had been flying prospectors and planters, among others, to various sites in the remote Amazon-Orinoco country. Over coffee in a café we developed the idea of starting an express-passenger operation in what is now called Indonesia.

From previous experience I knew there were people willing to pay premium prices for speedy transportation and delivery of express or freight to places where boats rarely called. There appeared to be enough small but valuable cargo around, in addition to passengers, to allow us to show a profit—at least on paper.

But before we did more than dream about it, my stories

began selling to the action pulp magazines back home and I elected to give all my attention to my writing. But I never did drop this whole idea entirely, for I created Turk Madden, who did tramp piloting for a living.

As men who spent a lot of time on the waterfront when not airborne, it was inevitable that Madden, Thorne, and Cowan would be drawn into the intrigue of World War II. For they trafficked information as well as people and cargo, and to those of us who have worked along the docks of the world, there is little information that can be kept secret for very long. If you're interested and reasonably alert you usually know what cargo is being shipped where and often can figure out why.

Many of us working dockside or as seamen in the East Indies in the late thirties got our first hint of what Germany and Japan were planning for the world when groups of their citizens began showing up unexpectedly in some of the smaller outlying ports. Were they stockpiling supplies for future raiders? Were they checking harbors, coves, and river mouths that might be used by merchant raiders? But once men started unloading unusually large shipments of sensitive Japanese and German cargo, we suspected a more disturbing motivation for their presence.

The more resourceful intelligence agents, like my Steve Cowan character, often get their best information not through subterfuge but just by listening in the right places. I was able to write about pocket submarines in a story about the East Indies, which I'll include in another collection, two years before the vessels first appeared at Pearl Harbor because early word had leaked out about them in the Pacific ports I visited. There are few secrets when men who do the work talk together, and I observed a lot of listeners as well as did a lot of listening myself back then.

I'm reminded of the time my small ship got the better of a large German freighter, which, typically, was discharging cargo but taking on very little. One of their seamen defected and came aboard our ship looking for a job. We were short-handed so we took him on. When they came looking for him we had him in the shaft alley, where they did not think to look. There was considerable discussion over him, and our captain was ashore several times talking to our consul, but when we sailed he was still aboard.

Preparing these stories for publication brought back a lot of old memories of other times. I almost wish I was back there on the waterfront again with the smell of the sea, tar, and spoiling fruit. I liked those off-the-end-of-the-world seaports like Gorontalo, Amurang, Hollandia, Port Moresby, and Broome as they used to be. I liked the people who inspired these stories just as they were, too. I wish some of them were still around to talk to and learn from. But I believe we will surely find their descendants mining on the moon and Mars, capturing asteroids, or finding the remnants of other lives at the outer limits of the solar system in the century to come.

AUTHOR'S NOTE
Night Over the Solomons

This story concerns the discovery of a Japanese base on the island of Kolombangara in the Solomons during World War II. Shortly after my story was published the Navy discovered this Japanese base of which I had written. I am sure my story had nothing to do with its discovery and doubt if the magazine in which it was published had reached the South Pacific at the time.

My decision to locate a Japanese base on Kolombangara was not based upon any inside information but upon simple logic. We had troops fighting on Guadalcanal. If the Japanese wished to harass our supply lines, where would they locate their base?

From my time at sea I had a few charts and I dug out the one on the Solomons. Kolombangara was the obvious solution. There was a place where an airfield could be built, a deep harbor where ships could bring supplies and lie unnoticed unless a plane flew directly over the harbor, which was well hidden. No doubt the Japanese had used the same logic in locating their base and the Navy in discovering it.

My story, however, offers an interesting coincidence. It offers two of them, in fact.

The lead character, an American named Mike Thorne, reaches shore from a torpedoed ship. My story was published in 1943. On January 31, that same year, Capt. Jefferson DeBlanc shot down three Japanese planes and was himself shot down, bailing out just above the water and injuring his back and legs. With the aid of his life jacket he swam to shore on Kolombangara.

On August 2 of that same year a young man named Jack Kennedy, his PT boat sunk at sea, made it to shore with some shipmates on one of several islets off the coast of Kolombangara.

Sometimes the imagination precedes reality.

NIGHT OVER THE SOLOMONS

He was lying face down under the mangroves about forty feet back from the sea on the southwest side of Kolombangara Island in the Solomons.

For two hours he had been lying without moving a muscle while two dozen Japanese soldiers worked nearby, preparing a machine-gun position.

Where he lay there were shadows, and scattered driftwood. He was concealed only by his lack of movement, although the outline of his body was blurred by broken timber and some odds and ends of rubbish, drifted ashore.

Now, the soldiers worked farther away. He believed they would soon move on. Then, and then only, would he dare to move. To be found, he knew, meant instant death.

He was dressed only in a ragged shirt, and the faded serge pants hastily donned in his escape from the sinking ship. The supply ship had been bombed and sunk in Blackett Strait, en route to Guadalcanal. If there were other survivors, he had seen none of them.

That he had lived while others died was due to one thing, and one thing only—he was, first and last, a fighting man, with the fighting man's instinct for timed, decisive action.

He was not, he reflected, much of a soldier. He was too strongly an individualist for that. He liked doing things his own way, and his experience in China and elsewhere had proved it a good way.

He lay perfectly still. The sun was hot on his back, and beneath him the sand was hot. The shadow that had offered partial concealment had moved now, the sun shone directly down upon him. From his memory of the mangrove's arch he

3

believed he would lack the shadow no more than fifteen minutes. It might be too long.

Yet he dare not move. He was not in uniform, and could be killed as a spy. But the Japanese were not given to hair splitting on International Law. He was ashore on an island supposedly deserted, an island where the Japanese were apparently building a strong position.

Overhead, a plane suddenly moaned in a dive, then came out, and from the corner of his eye he saw it skim the ragged edge of the crater and vanish.

That Japanese was a flier. Say what one would about them, they could fly.

In his mind he studied the situation. Soon, he could move. When he moved he must know exactly where he was going and what he intended to do. There must be no hesitation.

Behind him lay the sea. It promised nothing. Before him, the jungle. He had no need to study the island, for he knew it like the back of his hand. He hadn't visited Kolombangara for several years, but his memory was excellent.

Two rounded ridges lifted toward a square-topped crater. The crater itself was the end of an imposing ridge of volcanic rock, not far from Shoulder Hill. Both ridge and hill extended downward from one side of what had once been an enormous crater that had at some distant time been ripped asunder, exposing the entrails of the mountain.

Now, jungle growth had healed the surface of the wound, leaving the riven crater divided into two magnificent gullies whose walls lifted five thousand feet above the sea. Their lofty pinnacles lost themselves in the clouds, towering above a scene majestic in its savage splendor.

Those rugged slopes offered concealment. They might offer food. It was characteristic of Mike Thorne not to think of a weapon. He had his hands. When the time came he would take his weapon from the Japanese.

They would be concentrated near Bambari Harbor. Not large, but perfectly sheltered, it offered excellent concealment from all but close aerial reconnaissance. What supplies the Japanese would need must be landed there. That they were ready for trouble was obvious from their careful preparation of machine-gun and mortar positions at this spot. Here, if necessary, a landing could be effected.

Something big was in the wind. Obviously, this was intended as base for a sudden and terrific blow at the American flank. From here a mighty blow could be unleashed at the American forces on Guadalcanal and other Solomon positions. Somewhere on the island the Japanese had a secret landing field.

Suddenly, he tensed. Directly before him there was a stealthy movement in the jungle. A second later, ghostlike, he saw a Japanese soldier slide through the jungle. Even at the bare thirty feet that separated them, the man was all but invisible.

Fascinated by something he was stalking, the Japanese was crouched, staring ahead. He moved again, and vanished.

Mike scowled. What was this?

Something in the manner of the man told Thorne the soldier was closing in for a kill. His intended victim, being an enemy of the Japanese must be a friend of Thorne.

The American hesitated. To lie still was to remain safe. To interfere was to risk his own freedom or even his life.

Thorne moved. He left the ground in a swift, deadly rush that brought him to the edge of the jungle. Sliding into the dense cover, every sense alert, Mike's big hands opened, then closed. They were all he had, his only weapon.

Stealthily, he advanced. The Japanese had paused and was lifting his rifle. Then, surprisingly, the fellow lowered his gun and Mike, closing in, saw his teeth bare in an ugly grimace. Wetting his lips the Japanese moved forward.

In that instant, Mike saw the girl. She was not twenty feet from the Japanese, facing the opposite direction. She had paused, listening.

Mike lunged.

Catlike, the Japanese whirled, stabbing at Mike's throat with the bayonet.

Instantly, Thorne slapped the blade aside with an open hand and moving in, dropped the other over his opponent, at the same time hooking a heel to trip him. With a quick push, he spilled him and snatched the rifle away.

A shot rang out, and Mike wheeled to see two Japanese coming toward him on the jump. Dropping to one knee, Thorne fired, once, twice. Both men spilled to the ground.

*   *   *

Springing up, Mike was just in time to meet the bare-handed rush of the soldier he had disarmed. But as he jerked the bayonet up, it hung on a liana, and before he could free it, the Japanese had leaped upon him. Thorne staggered back, losing his grip on the rifle, and clawing desperately to get the man's hands free from his throat.

Fighting like madmen, they hit the ground hard. His opponent tried to knee him, but Mike rolled away, driving a powerful right to the man's midsection. The Japanese tried to squirm out, but Thorne was fighting savagely. He leaped up and rushed his enemy, smashing him against the bole of a huge tree with stunning impact.

The man's grip broke, and he fell away. Mike struck out viciously and the soldier crumpled.

"Quick! This way!" Glancing up, Thorne saw the girl beckoning, and out of the tail of his eye he glimpsed a rush of movement across the space where lately he had waited his chance.

Wheeling, he ran after the girl. Vaulting a fallen tree, he plunged into the brush. The girl ran swiftly, picking her ground with the skill of long familiarity.

Suddenly, she stopped. Holding up her hand for stillness, she began to worm swiftly through the jungle. Mike followed. This way, with their momentary start, they might elude the Japanese. The girl was working her way along the ridge, when Mike recalled the cavern.

"This way!" he whispered hoarsely. "Up!"

The girl hesitated, then followed. Mike Thorne took a path that led steadily upward, at times almost closing in around them. Behind, the sounds of pursuit increased, then suddenly died away. The Japanese were cautious now, but they were coming on.

Ruthless and determined, they would be relentless in pursuit. It had ceased to be a matter of hiding away until he could escape. By interfering he had sacrificed all possibility of that. Now it was a matter of a fight to the death.

Once, halting beneath a towering crag, he glanced at the girl. For the first time he realized how lovely she was. Despite the jungle, the desperation of their climb and the heat, she was beautiful.

He was suddenly conscious of his own appearance, the torn uniform and scuffed boots—his open shirt stained with perspiration and his hair, naturally curly now a black tangle over his dark, sun-browned face.

"What will we do now?" she asked. "I know Ishimaru. He'll never stop until we are both killed."

Thorne shrugged. "We can't run for long," he said. "We've got to fight."

"But we can't," the girl protested. "There are only two of us, and we are unarmed!"

Mike Thorne smiled grimly. "So what? No matter how small one's force there is always a place where attack can be effective. There's only one method of war in the last analysis. Only one winning method. Attack always. If you have a squad, and the enemy a regiment, you look for a spot where a squad can attack. Maybe there's a patrol you can knock off, maybe there's a sudden raid you can make.

"Hit hard and keep moving. It does the job every time. That's what we'll do. We've got to keep them so busy protecting themselves they can't take time to look for us properly.

"See, kid? They've got a secret base here. They are getting set for an attack on Guadalcanal. An attack now, from here, could do a terrific amount of damage. So they don't dare let anything happen here. We'll see that plenty happens."

Turning, he led the way up a steep mountain path. They were leaving the heavier jungle behind and worming a precarious way through a maze of gigantic boulders, enormous volcanic crags, and beds of lava. It was a strange, unbelievable world, a world of rocks that looked like frozen flame.

Suddenly they were in a gray fog layer, and Mike stopped, glancing back. They were in the low clouds now, over four thousand feet above the sea.

The girl came up to him. He glanced at her curiously.

"What in the world are you doing in these islands?" he demanded. "At a time like this?"

She smoothed her hair and looked at him.

"My father was here. He persisted in staying on, regardless of everything. But he told me that if the Japanese did come to the Solomons, he would leave Tulagi and come here. There was a place we both knew where he could hide. And he didn't believe they would bother with Kolombangara."

"That's just the trouble," Mike said grimly. "Nobody thinks they will. That still doesn't tell me how you got here."

"I flew. I've had my own plane for several years. I learned to fly in California, and after I returned here, it was easy for me to fly back and forth, to cruise among the islands. I was in Perth when the Japanese came, and they wouldn't let me come back after Daddy.

"Then, three days ago, I finally succeeded. I took off and landed here at Bambari Harbor, and when I went ashore, the Japanese were waiting for me. I got away, but they have the plane."

They moved on, working their way among the crags, still heading onward and upward. They left no trail on the lava, and the jumble of broken rock and blasted trees concealed them.

Once, on the very crest of the ancient crater, where the lip hung over the dizzy spaces below, they came upon a tangle of huge trees, dead and dried by sun and wind, great skeletonlike fingers of trees, the bones and wreckage of a forest. They were worn out and panting heavily when they reached the other side.

Then Mike Thorne saw what he was looking for, a curious white streak on the face of a great, leaning boulder. He walked toward it, skirted the boulder, and, without a word, squeezed into a narrow crack behind it. Following him, the girl saw him turn sharply to the left, in the passage, then to the right, then suddenly they stood in a small open place, green with soft grass. Beyond, the black entrance to a cave opened, and, from a crevice in the rock near the cave mouth, a trickle of water fell into a basin about as big as a washtub.

"You knew this was here?" she asked, staring about wonderingly. "But the water, where does it come from?"

"Seepage. It seeps down from a sort of natural reservoir on top of that peak. Rain collects there in a rock basin and seeps down here. There is always water."

"They would never find us here." She looked at him. "But what now? What will we do?"

"Sleep. We'll need rest. Tonight, I'm going back down the mountain."

"It would take hours!" she protested, glancing at the lowering sun.

"Not the way I'm going!" His voice was grim. "I'm going down the inside of the crater."

Memory of her one glimpse of that yawning chasm gripped her. The idea of anyone suspended over that awful space was a horror.

"But you can't! There's no way—"

"Yes, there is." He smiled at her. "I saw it once. I've often wondered if it could be done. Tonight, by moonlight, I'll find out." He smiled, and his teeth flashed white. "Say, what is your name, anyway? Mine's Mike Thorne."

She laughed. "I'm Jerry Brandon."

Hours later, she awakened suddenly. There was a stealthy movement in the cave, and then she saw Mike Thorne standing in the entrance. He bent over and drank at the spring, then straightened, tightening his belt. She moved swiftly beside him.

"Be careful," she whispered.

"Don't worry," he replied softly. He pressed her hand gently. "So long."

He moved off. One moment he was there beside her, then he was gone. Remembering that almost bottomless chasm, she shuddered.

Mike Thorne moved swiftly. He had no plan. He knew too little about the enemy dispositions to plan. He must make his reconnaissance and attack at one time.

When he reached the lip of the crater, he hesitated, drawing a deep breath. He knew the place. In the past, he had speculated on whether or not a strong, agile man could make it down to five thousand feet from that point.

Taking firm grasp on a rock, he lowered himself over the rim. For an instant his feet dangled in space. Carefully, he felt for the ledge he remembered. He found it, tested it briefly with his weight, then relaxed his grip and felt for a new hand hold on the edge itself.

Slowly, painstakingly, he worked his way down, the six-inch ledge of rock, feeling with feet and hands for each new hold.

On the way up the mountain he had thought much. Areas for

possible landing fields were few. Kolombangara was rough, and the best spot, if not the only spot, was on the floor of the crater itself. There was a chance that when he reached bottom he'd find himself at the edge of their field.

Suddenly, he was in complete blackness. Twisting his head. Mike saw the moon was under a cloud. From his memory of the cliff, he knew he had reached the most difficult point. Carefully, he felt over a toehold, found it, and reached out in the darkness. His hand felt along the bare rock, searching, searching.

A protruding corner of rock met his fingers. He gripped it, shifted his weight. The rock came loose.

For one awful, breathtaking instant, he grabbed wildly, then he felt himself falling.

He slid, grabbed out, felt a rock tear loose from his hand, and fell clear. He must have turned over at least three times before he struck with such force that it knocked the wind from him, then slid, and started to fall again. His hand, grasping wildly, caught a shrub. It pulled, then held.

Breathless, frightened, he hung over the void.

Around him was absolute silence. Slowly, majestically, the moon slid from behind the cloud. To his horror he saw the bush to which he clung had pulled out by the roots, and seemed suspended only by a few stronger roots that might give way at any moment.

Turning his head carefully, he glanced below. Nothing but blackness. The shrub gave a sickening sag, then held.

Moving cautiously, he felt with his toe. He found a toehold, not more than an inch of rock. Then another inch, and he let go with one hand. A heavy root thrust out from the face, and he took hold with a sigh of relief.

Almost a half hour later, he let himself down on the slope, then stepped into the brush. He had worked along silently through the jungle only a little way when he heard a clink of metal against metal. He froze. A Japanese sentry stood not twenty feet away, and beyond him bulked the dark body of a plane.

Mike Thorne flattened against the earth. The grass beneath him was damp. He crept softly nearer the sentry. The man turned rifle on guard, staring out into the dark toward him.

Mike lay still. Then the sentry shouldered his rifle and walked away.

Listening, Thorne could hear the man's feet recede, then stop, then start back. Mike moved forward and lay still.

The sentry drew near, paused, and turned away. Swiftly, Mike lunged. His left arm slid around the sentry's throat, crushing the bony part of the wristbone against the man's Adam's apple. His left hand grasped his own right wrist, and Mike gave a quick, hard jerk. The man's body threshed, then relaxed slowly. Grimly, Mike Thorne lowered the body to the ground.

When he straightened again, he carried a heavy-bladed knife. It was a smatchet, evidently taken from some British commando, or picked from the ground after a battle. The rifle he put aside.

Moving forward, he sniffed air heavy with the fumes of gasoline. He hesitated, then felt around. Several tins of gas stood about the plane. It was a Zero pursuit.

Deliberately, he opened the cans and poured one of them over the plane itself. His time was short. He knew the chances of discovery were increased immeasurably by every instant, yet he worked on.

A movement froze him to stillness. A Japanese sentry had stopped not fifty feet away and was staring toward him. The man stepped forward and spoke softly, inquiringly. Mike Thorne crouched, his lips a thin line along his teeth.

This was it. He could see it coming. Suddenly the Japanese jerked up his rifle. There was no hesitation. The man fired as the rifle came up, and the bullet smashed into the pile of cases beside Thorne. Instantly, Thorne lunged. The rifle cracked again, and a bullet whiffed by his cheek. The soldier lunged with the bayonet, and Mike felt the point tear through his sleeve, then he struck viciously with the smatchet.

Blood gushed from the side of the Japanese's neck, but the man scarcely staggered. He wheeled, dropping his rifle, and grabbed at Thorne's throat. Mike tried to pull away, slashing viciously at the sentry with the heavy knife.

The camp was in an uproar. Running men were coming from every direction. With a tremendous burst of strength, Mike hurled the sentry from him, struck a match, and dropped it into the gasoline.

The tower of flame leaped high into the sky behind him, but he had plunged into the brush. He was running wildly, desperately. Running so fast that he never saw the wire until it was too late. He plunged into it, tried to leap, but his foot hung and he fell forward. Desperately, he hurled himself to one side, trying to avoid the barbs. He fell flat, and his head struck one of the anchor pins. He felt the blow, but nothing more.

His eyes opened on a different world. Weird flames lit the sky, although they were dying down now. They wouldn't, he decided, be enough to attract help. It was too deep within the sheltering bulwarks of the crater.

He was bound to a tree, his right leg around the bole, the toe hooked under the left knee. The left leg was bent back under him. His arms were tied around the tree itself.

Mike's eyes were narrow with apprehension. He knew what this meant. In such a position, in a short time his legs would be paralyzed and helpless. If he were to escape, it must be now, at once. From the tail of his eye he could see enough to know that two planes had been burned, and a fair quantity of supplies.

Suddenly, a shadow loomed between the fire and himself. He tilted his head, and a stunning blow knocked it down again.

"So?" The voice was a hiss. "You?"

He looked up, brow wrinkled with anguish. Commander Ishimaru stared down at him. He remembered the man from an event on the coast of China. He forced a grin. "Sure, it's me, Mike Thorne. How's tricks?"

Ishimaru studied him.

"No change, I see," he said softly. "I am glad. You will break harder, my friend." He bowed, and his eyes glittered like obsidian in the firelight.

The Japanese officer studied him. "Where did you come from?" he went on. "How many are there? Why did you come here?"

"Side issue," Mike replied. "Doolittle and his boys are taking another sock at Tokyo. They sent me down here to keep you boys busy while the big show comes off. Doolittle is going to blast Tokyo to the ground and burn the Mikado in its ashes."

Ishimaru struck him viciously across the face. Once, twice. Then again.

"Better take a sock at a Yank when you can, Yellow Belly," Mike said, "you won't get many chances. Our boys are whipping the devil out of yours."

"You tell me how many, and where they are." Ishimaru's voice was level. "Otherwise, you burn."

"Go to the devil," Mike replied.

"You have ten minutes to decide." Ishimaru's voice was sharp. He spun on his heel and walked away.

Mike Thorne's lips tightened. His legs were already feeling their cramped position. The position alone would soon be torture enough, but the Japanese would not let it rest there. He knew only too well the fiendish tortures they could devise. Slivers of bamboo thrust under the fingernails and lighted, other things too ugly to mention. He had seen men after Japanese torture, and it had turned him sick. And Mike Thorne wasn't a man to be bothered easily.

If he was to escape, it must be now, at once. From the activity around the landing field he could see that the hour of attack was approaching. The wreckage of the two burned pursuit ships had been hurriedly cleared away. The other planes were being fueled and readied for the takeoff. From his position his view was limited, but there were at least fifty Zeros on the landing field.

More, the Japanese were wheeling attack bombers from concealed positions. In the confusion he was almost forgotten.

Desperately, he tried to pull himself erect. It was impossible. The cramped position of his legs was slowly turning them numb. He strained against the ropes that bound him, but without success.

His arms were not only bound around the tree, but were higher than his head, and tied there. By pressing the inside of his arms against the tree trunk he succeeded in lifting himself a bare inch. It did no good and only caused the muscles in his legs to cramp.

Trying to get the ropes that bound his wrists against the tree bark did him no good. He sawed but only succeeded in chafing his wrists.

A movement in the shadow of some packing cases startled him. Suddenly, to his astonishment, Jerry Brandon emerged from behind the cases. She walked across to him, unhurriedly, then bent over his wrists.

"Get out of here!" he snapped, and was astonished by the fierceness of his voice. "They'll get you! These devils—!"

"Be still!" Jerry sawed at the ropes, and suddenly his wrists were free, then his feet. Slowly, carefully, she helped him up.

"Beat it," he said tersely. "You've done enough. If they catch you, death will be too easy for you. I can't run now. I doubt if I can even walk."

Her arm about him, he tottered a few steps and almost fell. The pain in his legs was excruciating. Suddenly he saw the smatchet he'd had lying on a case beside some rifles. He staggered to the case and picked it up. They each took a rifle.

A Japanese dropped a sack to the ground at the nearest plane and started to turn. He saw them, hesitated, then started forward.

"This is it," Mike said. "Get out of here. I'll get away now. Anyway, no use both of us being caught."

The soldier halted, stared, then turned to shout. Mike Thorne lifted the rifle and fired. His first bullet struck the man in the head and he pitched over. The second smashed into the plane.

Jerry Brandon was beside him, and she fired also. Slowly, they began to back away, taking advantage of every bit of cover, firing as they retreated. A bullet smashed into a tree trunk beside Mike, and he stepped back, loading the rifle again.

They were almost to the brush, and turning, he started for it in a tottering run. Jerry fired another shot, then ran up alongside him. Together they fled into the brush.

Behind them the field was in a turmoil. The escape had come without warning, the sudden firing within the camp had added to the confusion, and it had been a matter of minutes before anyone was aware of just what had happened.

But now a line of soldiers fanned out and started into the jungle.

Mike Thorne stopped, wetting his bruised lips. This was going to be tough. The Japanese would cut them off from his trail up the mountain. They knew where they had lost him before and this time would take care to prevent that. Furthermore, they were closer to the path up the mountain than he.

*   *   *

Worse, the ascent of the precipice down which he had come would be impossible for him in his present condition. And it was a cinch Jerry would never be able to make it.

Despite the little he had been able to do, the Japanese would go ahead with their attack, and soon. That he knew. He had no idea what the disposition of forces was on the American side. That this massing of Japanese forces had been carried out in great secrecy, he knew. Obviously, it would come as a complete surprise to Guadalcanal. Such a raid now might seriously cripple the South Pacific war effort of the Allies.

His own problem was serious, but there was another, greater than that. Death for himself, even for Jerry Brandon, was a small thing compared to the fearful destruction of a sudden, successful attack on grounded planes and ships at anchor. The loss of life would be terrific. But what to do? What could two people do in such a case, far from means of communication. . . .

But were they? The idea came suddenly.

Instantly, he knew it would work. It was the only way, the only possible way. Possible? He smiled wryly into the darkness. Was it possible? It meant climbing the cliff in the darkness, climbing along the sheer face, feeling for handholds, risking death at every second. It meant doing what only a moment before he had said was impossible.

They slid swiftly through the jungle, but now, taking the girl's hand, he chose a new path. He was going to the cliff.

Suddenly, the girl's grip tightened.

"Mike, you're not going to . . . ?"

"Yes, I am," he said quietly. "Something big's coming off. I'm not going to sit by and see the enemy close in on those boys on Guadalcanal. Not those swell guys."

"But what can you do?" Jerry protested. "Getting up that cliff won't help. And I can't climb it, even in daytime."

"You aren't going to," he told her. "I know a cave in the rocks down below. You can stay there. I'm going up, somehow, some way. If I should fall, you'll have to try. This is no time to talk about men or women or weaker sexes. Up on that peak there is heaped-up forest, forest dead and parched by sun and wind, rotting in places, but mostly just dry. We've got to set fire to it."

"Could they see it from there, Mike? It's so far!"

He shrugged. "You can see a candle twelve miles from a

plane on a dark night. I'm hoping some scout will sight this flame. It should be visible for miles and miles."

"But won't the Japanese put it out?" Jerry protested.

"They'll try." He laughed softly. "But I've still got that rifle. You have another. We've some ammunition. We'll lie in the brush, or I will, and when they start into the firelight . . . Baby, the hunting will be good tonight!"

Yet when he reached the foot of the cliff he stopped dead still. Suddenly, despite the oppressive heat, he felt cold. Above him, looming in the darkness, the gigantic precipice towered toward the stars. Somehow, along the face of that awful cliff, he had climbed down, feeling his way. Now he must go back.

A slip meant an awful death on the jagged rocks below. Yet not to climb meant that many men would die, brave men who would perish in a world of rending steel and blasting, searing flame.

His hands found a crevice, and he started. Inch by inch, he felt his way along, the awful void growing below him as he mounted upward. Rocks crumbled under his fingers, roots gave way, he clung, flattened against the rock as though glued to it, living for the moment only. His flesh damp with cold sweat, his skin alive, the nerves sensing every roughness in the rock.

Time and again he slipped, only to catch hold, then mount higher. A long time later, his clothing soaked, his fingers torn and bleeding, he crawled over the ridge and lay face down on the rock. His pounding heart seemed to batter the solid surface beneath him, his lungs gasped for air, his muscles felt limp.

"So . . . I was correct."

The voice was sibilant, cold. Mike Thorne's eyes opened wide, suddenly alert. Ishimaru's voice broke into the feeling of failure, of utter depression that swept over him. "I knew you would try it, American. So foolish to try to outwit Ishimaru. You see, I knew what you would think. I remembered this mountain, too."

Mike knew he was covered, knew a move meant death. Yet he moved suddenly and with violence. He had drawn his hands back to his sides unconsciously, and with a sudden push up he hurled himself forward against the soldier's legs.

A gun roared in his ears, and he felt the man go down before him. He lunged to his feet, and Ishimaru, wild with fury, fired from the ground. A searing flame scorched the side of Thorne's face, and then he dove head first onto him.

Like a cat, the Japanese officer rolled away. He came up quickly and, as Mike lunged in, grabbed at his wrist. But Mike was too wise in the ways of judo, swung away, and whipped a driving right to the chin. The officer went down, hard.

Feet rushed, and Mike saw a man swinging at him with a rifle butt. He dropped in a ball at the man's feet, and the fellow tripped and fell headlong, rolling over the edge of the cliff. The Japanese made one wild, futile grab with his fingers, then vanished, his scream ringing into the heavens.

Mike's rifle had fallen from his shoulders where it had been slung. Now he grabbed it up and fired two quick shots, then dove into the brush. He staggered through the jungle toward the place he had chosen to start the fire. Heedless of danger, he dropped to his knees, scraped together some sticks, and with paper from his pocket, lit the fire.

A shot smacked dully into the log near him, and he rolled over. The flame took hold, then a volley of shots riddled the brush around him. By a miracle he was unhurt. A Japanese came leaping into the growing firelight, and Mike's rifle cracked. The soldier fell headlong. Another, and another shot.

The flame caught in a heap of dead branches, flared, and leaped high. In a roaring holocaust, it swirled higher and higher, mounting a fast crescendo of unbelievable fury toward the dark skies. The scene around was lit by a weird light, and into it came the Japanese.

Desperately, yet methodically, making every shot count, Mike Thorne began to fire. He sprang to his feet, rushed, changed position, opened fire again. A bullet stung him along the arm, something struck his leg a solid blow. He raised to one knee, blood trickling from a cut on his scalp, and fired again.

Then, suddenly, another rifle opened fire across the clearing. Taken on the flank, the advancing enemy hesitated, then broke for the jungle.

Suddenly, over the roar of the fire, Mike heard the roar of motors. Their planes, taking off!

He saw them mount, swing around, then a bomb dropped.

He heard it one instant before it exploded and hurled himself flat. The earth heaved under him, and the fire lifted and scattered in all directions, but roared on.

Then out of the night he heard the high-pitched whine of a diving plane, and the night was lit with the insane lightning of tracer gone wild, while over his head the sky burst into a roaring, chattering madness of sound.

Battle! Planes had come, and there was fighting up there in the darkness. He rolled over, swearing in a sullen voice, swearing in sheer relief that his warning had been successful. He fired at a Japanese soldier, saw the flames catch hold anew, and then as his rifle clicked on an empty chamber, he lunged erect, hauling out the smatchet.

Suddenly, something white loomed in the sky, and then a man hit the ground beside him. It was a paratrooper! An American! Then the night was filled with them, and Mike staggered toward the man. A dozen had landed when the Japanese charged.

Mike shouted hoarsely, and whirling, sprang toward them, his face weirdly lit by the roaring flames, his smatchet cleaving the night in a gleaming streak of steel. His first blow cut through a Japanese arm like a knife through butter, and suddenly they were all around him.

Then the paratroopers hit in a solid wedge, more came, and the Japanese began to scatter.

A shouting officer grabbed Mike's arm. "What is it? Where the devil are they coming from?"

Mike roared the information into his ear, and the officer began a crisp recital of the information into the radio.

A plane roared over, then explosions came from the chasm below, the night changed from the bright rattle of machine-gun fire to the solemn, unceasing thunder of big bombs as the bombers shuttled back and forth, releasing their eggs over the enemy field.

Mike staggered back, feeling his numbed leg. It wasn't bleeding. Evidently a stick knocked against his leg by a bullet, or a stone. He turned, dazed.

Jerry Brandon came running toward him. "Mike! Are you all right?"

"Sure," he said. "Where . . . ?"

"I came up the trail. I thought maybe I could make it, and when the fighting started up there, I got through all right."

The Army officer walked back through the smoke and stopped beside Mike. "This is a good night's work, friend," he said. "Who are you?"

Briefly, Mike told him. The officer looked curiously at Jerry. Mike explained, and the officer nodded. "Yes," he said dryly, "we heard about you. Incidentally, your father's safe. He got into Henderson Field last night."

They turned away. Mike looked at Jerry, smiling wearily. "Lady," he said, "tired as I am, I can still wonder at finding a girl like you in the Solomons. If there wasn't a war on . . ." He looked at her again. "After all," he said thoughtfully, "what's a war between friends?"

Jerry laughed. "I think you could handle the war, too," she said.

AUTHOR'S NOTE
Mission to Siberut

Even in those knockabout years I was trying to write, but the few stories I found time to do were returned unsold, some of them following me about for months. Some were lost, and along with them much poetry that I mailed off that never found a publisher or a return address for me.

Yet wherever I went I tried to learn, to store memories of what lay ahead. The western shores of Sumatra were experienced but briefly, long enough to soak up some atmosphere, to observe and to study the sailing directions, and to ask questions of those who had been there before.

The duration of one's visit is less important than the intensity of one's observation and study. Siberut is one of the Mentawi island group, an island about sixty miles long by twenty broad, a high, forested place. Emma Haven, the port of Padang, was the nearest of any size at all. The natives on Siberut were wary, but seemed willing to be friendly.

Siberut was not on the tourist routes. To get there you had to have reason. The tourist boats go to the obvious places, where there are comfortable accommodations, where John and Mary can see the same things seen by Henry and Ethel. Off the beaten track the things you most wish to know are not repeated to you because the local people take them for granted.

MISSION TO SIBERUT

Steve Cowan cut the throttle and went into a steep glide. He glanced at his instruments and swore softly. If he made it this time, he would need a rabbit's foot in each pocket. Landing an amphibian on a patch of water he had seen but once several years before, and in complete darkness! But war was like that.

The dark hump beneath him would be Tanjung Sigep, if his calculations were correct. Close southward was Labuan Bajau Bay. The inner bay, visible only from the air, was the place he was heading for. It was almost a mile long, about a thousand yards wide, and deep enough. But picking it out of the black, jungle-clad island of Siberut on a moonless night was largely a matter of instruments, guesswork, and a fool's luck.

Cowan saw the gleam of water. Guessing at four or five feet, he leveled off and drew back gently on the stick. The hull took the water smoothly, and the ship lost flying speed rapidly.

At one place, there was about an acre of water concealed behind a tongue of land overgrown with casuarina trees. Taxiing the amphibian around the tongue of land, Cowan anchored it safely in the open water behind the casuarinas. When he finished, the first streaks of dawn were in the sky.

Mist was rising from the jungle, and on the reef outside Labuan Bajau Bay he could hear the roar and pound of surf. There would be heavy mist along the reef, too, lifting above that pounding sea. Cowan opened a thermos bottle and drank the hot coffee, taking the chill of the night from his bones. . . .

Two days ago in Port Darwin, Major Garnett had sent for him. Curious, he responded at once. Garnett had come to the point immediately.

23

"You're a civilian, Cowan. But you volunteered for duty, and you've flown over most of the East Indies. Know anything about Siberut?"

"Siberut?" Cowan was puzzled. "A little. I've been on all the Mentawi Islands. Flew over from Emma Haven on the coast of Sumatra."

Garnett nodded.

"No Europeans, are there?" he asked.

Cowan hesitated.

"Not to speak of. The natives are timid and friendly enough, but they can be mighty bad in a pinch. Villages are mostly black inland. It's heavily jungled, with only a few plantations. There are, I think, a few white men."

"How about that trouble of yours some years back? Weren't they white men?" Garnett asked keenly.

Steve Cowan chuckled.

"You check up on a guy, don't you? But that was no trouble. It was a pleasure. That was Besi John Mataga. He's a renegade."

"I know." Major Garnett nodded. "Furthermore, we understand he is negotiating with the enemy. That's why I've sent for you."

He leaned forward.

"It's like this Cowan. Intelligence has learned that fifty Messerschmitt 110s were flown from Tripoli to Dakar across the Sahara. They were loaded on a freighter heading for Yokohama. War broke out, and temporarily the freighter was cut off from Japan.

"Just what happened then, we only know from one of the crew, who was supposedly drowned. He got to us and reported that several of the crew, led by the chief mate, murdered the captain and took over the ship.

"The chief mate had some idea of striking a bargain with the Japanese. He'd claimed the ship was injured and that he could tell them where it was—for a price."

"And the mate is John Mataga, is that it?" Cowan asked.

"Exactly. Mataga had signed on under an assumed name, but was dealing with the Japanese as himself. Naturally, the freighter had to be hidden until a deal was struck. Our advices

are that the deal is about to go through. Of course, I needn't
tell you what those fifty Messerschmitts would mean to Japan."

"No." Cowan frowned. "Plane for plane we're much better
than they, even though we're badly outnumbered. But those
Messerschmitts would be tough to handle."

"That's it," Garnett agreed. "So they must never reach Japanese hands. They must be found and destroyed—and we
know exactly where they are!"

"Off Siberut?"

"Yes. Lying in Labuan Bajau Bay. You know it?"

"You bet." Cowan sat up. "What do I do and when do I
start?"

"You understand the situation," Garnett said. "We can't
spare the pilots for an attack. Indeed, we haven't planes enough.
But one ship, flown by a man who knew the locality, might slip
through. It's one chance in a thousand!"

Cowan shrugged.

"That makes the odds about right," he said. "You want that
freighter blown up?"

"Yes." Garnett nodded vigorously. "You've had no bombing
experience, so we can't trust to that. You must land, and . . ."

But that had been two days ago.

The first night, Steve Cowan had flown the amphibian to a
tiny inlet on the south coast of Java, where he remained all
day, hidden from hostile scouting planes. Then when darkness
fell, he took off again. Time and again he had narrowly missed
running into the enemy. Once, south of Bali, he had come out
of a cloud facing a lone Japanese plane.

He recognized it instantly. It was a Kawasaki 93, a bomber-
reconnaissance plane. In the same instant, he banked steeply
and sharply and fired a burst at its tail as it shot by him.

Cowan had the faster ship and could have escaped. But he
was conscious of nothing but the realization that if the pilot
broke free, it would be only a matter of minutes before speedy
pursuit ships would be hunting him down.

His turn had brought him around on the enemy's tail,
and he gunned his own ship. The Kawasaki tried an Immelmann
and let go a burst of fire as it whipped back over in the tight
turn. But Cowan was too close behind for the pilot's fire to
reach him.

He pulled his ship up so steeply he was afraid it would stall, but then he flattened out. For an instant the Kawasaki was dead in his sights.

Cowan's burst of fire smashed the Japanese's tail assembly into a stream of fragments. But their crew was game. They tried to hit Cowan with a burst from the observer's gun.

Cowan saw the stream of tracer go by. Then he banked steeply and swung down in a long dive after the falling ship, pumping a stream of steel-jacketed bullets into his target. Suddenly the Kawasaki burst into flame. An instant later, a red, roaring mass, it struck the sea with a terrific smash.

The entire fight had lasted less than a minute. Cowan pulled back on his stick and shot upward, climbing until he saw the altimeter at sixteen thousand feet. Then he had leveled off and headed straight for Siberut.

Cowan drank the coffee slowly, then ate a bar of chocolate. It would be daylight in a matter of minutes, he knew. Beyond the clump of casuarinas on the shore would be the renegade freighter. Beyond the trees, and probably a mile away.

Carefully Cowan stowed his gear, then checked his guns. He was carrying two of them, a .45 Colt automatic for a belt-gun and a .380. The smaller gun was strapped to his leg inside his trousers. There was a chance he might need an ace in the hole.

The explosive he'd brought along for the job was ready. It had been carefully prepared two days before by one of the best demolition experts in Australia.

Cowan made his way ashore through the mangroves that grew down close to his anchorage. Then he swung down from the trees and walked along the sand under the casuarinas.

Besi John Mataga would not leave the freighter unguarded. There would be some of the crew aboard. And if Steve Cowan knew Besi John, the crew members would be the scum of the African waterfronts where they had been recruited.

How he was to handle that part of it, Cowan didn't know. You could rarely plan a thing like that; so much depended on chance. You knew your objective, and you went there ready to take advantage of any chance you got.

The Japanese would be hunting the ship. They wouldn't pay off to Besi John without having a try for it. But on the other hand, they couldn't afford to delay for long. The planes were needed too badly, with streams of new Curtiss, Bell, and Lockheed pursuit jobs pouring into Australia.

Cowan halted under the heavy branches of a casuarina. The outer harbor was open before him. There, less than a half mile away, was the *Parawan*, a battered freighter of Portuguese registry.

It was at least possible, even if improbable, that Besi John did not know of the inner harbor. In any case, no large ship could possibly negotiate the channel without great risk. The entrance, about two hundred yards wide, was shoal water for the most part and out of sight behind the point of casuarinas.

The *Parawan* lay in about sixteen fathoms, Cowan judged, remembering the soundings of the outer harbor. On the shore close by was a hut, where traders used to barter for rotan and other wood products.

Moving along the point toward the mainland, Steve Cowan studied the freighter from all angles. He would have to get aboard by night; there was no other way. In any event, it wasn't going to be easy.

Keeping under cover of the jungle, Cowan worked his way along the shore. Several times he paused to study the sandy beach. Once he walked back under the roots of a giant ficus tree, searching about in the darkness.

A ripple in the still water nearby sent a shiver along his spine. He watched the ominous snout and drew back further from the water's edge.

"Crocs," he said. "Crocs in the streams and sharks in the bay."

Coming to the bank of a small stream, he hesitated, then walked upstream. Finally he found what he sought. In a clump of thick brush under the giant roots of a mangrove, he found a dugout.

Cowan had known it would be there. The natives would want a boat on this bay, and all the boats would not be upstream at the villages. He was going to need that dugout. The bay, like all the waters around Sumatra, was teeming with sharks.

Walking along the shore under cover of the trees, Cowan stopped abruptly. He had been about to step out into a clearing. There in the open space was the hut where the traders used to meet. Two men stood in front of it.

*   *   *

Besi John Mataga had his back to him, but Steve Cowan
recognized the man at once. No one else had that thick neck
and those heavy shoulders. The other man was younger, with a
lean, hard face and a Heidelberg scar. Cowan's eyes narrowed.

"They won't find this place!" Mataga said harshly. "It ain't so
easy spotted. If they do, they'll never get away. We got our
own spies around here."

"You'd better have." The stranger's voice was crisp. "And
don't underestimate the Aussies and the Yanks. They might
locate this place. It must be known to other people."

"Sure." Besi John shrugged. "Sure it is, Donner. But it ain't
the sort of place they'd figure on. White men, they never come
here. One did once, but he won't again."

"Who was that?" Donner demanded.

"A guy named Cowan. I had a run-in with him once out
there on the beach. I whipped the tar out of him."

"You lie!" Steve Cowan muttered to himself.

He studied Donner. Instinct warned him that here was an
even more dangerous opponent than Besi John. Mataga was a
thug—this man had brains.

"I'm giving the Japanese just forty-eight hours!" Donner
snapped. "They either talk turkey or I'll deal with somebody
else. I might start out for myself."

"They'll talk," Mataga chuckled "Birdie Wenzel knows how
to swing a deal. They'll pay off like he wants them to, and
plenty. Then we'll tell them where the ship is, and pull out—
but fast."

"What about them?" Donner said. He jerked a thumb over
his shoulder. "You still think the old man is good for some
cash?"

Mataga shrugged.

"I'm goin' to work on him. He knows where the dough is.
It's hid aboard that ship, and he knows where. He'll talk before
I get through with him!"

The two men turned and walked out to a dinghy where
several surly-looking seamen waited. They got in and shoved
off.

Cowan studied the hut. Now whom had Donner meant by
"them"?

While Cowan mulled it over, a husky seaman came around the corner of the hut, a rifle in the hollow of his arm. He said something through the door of the hut, and then laughed at the reply. He sat down against the wall, rifle across his lap.

Cowan stood half behind the bole of a huge tree and studied the situation anew. As long as that man remained where he was, there was no chance that a dugout could reach the freighter unobserved. The seaman was not only guarding whoever was in the hut but watching the ship as well. Even on the darkest night, it would be difficult to get away from shore without being seen.

Cowan circled around the hut. When he was behind it, he straightened up deliberately and walked toward it. Just as he stopped against the wall, he heard a light step. Wheeling, Cowan found himself facing a slender, hatchet-faced man with a rifle.

The fellow grinned, showing blackened stumps of teeth. Cowan did not hesitate. Dropping his left hand, he grabbed the rifle barrel and wrenched so hard that he jerked it free before the man's finger could squeeze the trigger.

Pulled off balance, the man fell forward into a smashing right uppercut to the wind. As he went down, Cowan struck him with the butt of his own rifle. He fell like a log and lay still.

Cowan wheeled, his breath coming hard. He was just in time. The big fellow he had seen on guard in front came around the side of the hut. Steve Cowan gave no warning, but struck viciously.

He was too anxious, and the punch missed. He caught a glancing blow from the other's rifle and went to his knees. Blinded with pain, he nevertheless lunged forward and grabbed the man by the knees. The fellow struck again. Cowan rolled free, lashing out with a short blow that landed without much force. Both men got up at once.

The big fellow's eyes flashed angrily. He rushed in, swinging wildly. Cowan lashed out himself, but caught one on the side of the head. The guard missed a vicious kick as Steve Cowan fell.

But the Yank was up quickly, and breathing hard. Steadying down, he met the rush with a hard right. The big fellow was fighting savagely, and apparently he had not considered a yell for help. Cowan knew he must get him, must knock the man out or kill him before he could shout.

It was more than a fight to win. It was more than a fight for mere life—although Cowan knew to lose meant death. It was a fight for all the lives that might be lost if those fifty crated pursuit ships out there got into Japanese hands.

The guard charged again, trying to close with him. Cowan struck with a short left to the face, then smashed a hard right to the wind. The guard lunged again. Cowan's left speared his mouth. Then the Yank drove in close, his big shoulders swaying with the rhythm of his punches.

The guard staggered, tried then to shout. But Cowan's rock-like fist smashed his lips again. The man went down, falling into a left hook that knocked him to the sand.

Cowan fell on him instantly and tied his hands behind his back. Then he bound his feet. Panting with the exertion, the Yank started for his first opponent. One glance was enough. The man was dead.

Picking up the guard's rifle, Cowan threw the other man's weapon into the brush. Then he sauntered around the hut, keeping his head down. In build, the Yank was not unlike the man he had tied up. If observed with glasses from the freighter, he might pass to an unsuspecting watcher for the guard. That individual was heavier, but it was not too noticeable at a distance.

Once around the shack Steve Cowan stepped warily inside, fearing there might still be a third guard. But there were only two people—an elderly man and a girl, both bound to chairs. They stared at him anxiously.

Hastily Cowan knelt and freed them. He glanced then at the man.

"You, I take it, are the captain of that ship out there," he said.

The man nodded, questioning gratitude in his eyes.

"Name of Forbes, Ben Forbes. This is my niece, Ruanne. Had a mutiny off the Cape. Left Dakar for Saigon, French Indochina, the sixth of last December. Mr. Mataga—he told me his name was Long—brought us in here after a week's layover at Amsterdam. The island, you know."

Cowan stepped back into the doorway.

"You'll have to stay in here until dark. I think they are watching. They'll believe I'm your guard."

"What happened to him?" Ruanne asked suddenly. It was the first attempt she had made to speak.

"He had a little trouble out back," Cowan said dryly. "He's tied up. There was another man, too."

"That was Ford. The big fellow is Sinker Powell. They were in the black gang," Captain Forbes explained.

"Ford's not going to be in any black gang again," Cowan said quietly. "The Sinker is still around, though."

Forbes couldn't yet contemplate his release.

"Who are you?" he asked. "Turning us loose, maybe I shouldn't ask, but—"

The Yank shrugged.

"Why not? The name is Steve Cowan. I'm a flyer. Commercial, not Army. To make it less formal, I'm a tramp flyer. I carry cargo, passengers, anything and anywhere."

"You'll help me take back my ship?" Forbes pleaded.

"Take it back?" Cowan gave him a sidelong glance. "Cap, there must be twenty men aboard there."

"Are you afraid?" Ruanne looked at him quietly, her eyes inscrutable. "You don't look like a man who would be afraid. But I could be wrong."

Cowan grinned, feeling his face tenderly.

"I only wear this blood on my head when I meet ladies. Anyway"—he looked at Forbes—"I couldn't help you, Captain. I'm a guy who doesn't beat around the bush. I came here for one reason, to blow your ship sky high, and blown up it will be before I leave this island.

"You can help me, though. If you don't want to, all I ask is that you stay out of my way. I've got a plane, and when this is over I'll fly you out."

Forbes glared at him.

"Blow up my ship? Are you crazy, man! There's cargo aboard that ship for Saigon, and that's where it'll go!"

"No," Steve Cowan replied quietly, "it goes no further. There are planes aboard that ship for Japan."

Forbes' eyes narrowed.

"A crank, eh? Young man, if you have an idea you can start

injuring Japan by sinking my ship, you're all wrong. You sound like one of these 'Yellow Peril' loudmouths. You talk like a blatherskite! Why, that's all nonsense! I lived in Japan, and—"

Cowan lighted a cigarette. When he dropped the match, he leaned his shoulder back against the wall.

"Cap," he said slowly, "when did you say you left Dakar?"

"On December sixth. Why? What has that to do with—"

"Wait a minute, Uncle Ben." Ruanne's eyes were on Cowan. "He wants to say something."

"You left Dakar on December sixth," Cowan repeated slowly. "On the morning of December seventh, the Japanese raided the Pearl Harbor naval base. Then they invaded the Philippines, attacked Malaya, took Singapore, Balik Papan, Palembang, Menado, Rabaul, and the whole Dutch East Indies. The islands in this part of the world are filled with their ships and planes.

"The United States Fleet struck back at the Marshall Islands. Our planes have begun action from Australia. You are right on the edge of the biggest war in history!"

Captain Ben Forbes stared at him, unbelieving.

"I—I don't believe it!" he gasped finally. "Unless Mataga bribed my radio operator to keep me in the dark. I never trusted him much."

"There's your answer," Steve said slowly. "Cap, your freighter out there has fifty Messerschmitt pursuit ships for the Japanese. Those planes can mean many lives lost, much equipment destroyed. They can, for a time and in a few places, give the Japanese equality or superiority in the air. It might be at the crucial spot.

"I know what a man's ship means to him, Cap," Cowan added. "But this is big. It's bigger than any of our lives, bigger than any of our jobs. I was sent here to see that that freighter is blown up. I'm going to do it."

"He's right, Uncle Ben," Ruanne said softly. "He's very right."

All through the day they waited, discussing the ship, the crew and the chances there would be. Sinker Powell lay bound and gagged, but he glared furiously and struggled.

Captain Forbes paced the hut.

"I don't like it!" he said finally. "You're going aboard that ship alone. If they jump you—"

"If they do," Cowan said grimly, "it will be up to you, Cap. That cargo must be destroyed."

Forbes hesitated suddenly.

"There's a lot of casing-head gas aboard," he said thoughtfully. "It's stowed amidships in steel drums. There's a tank aft we carried gasoline in, but it's empty now. I was going to have it cleaned when we got to Saigon. But you might dump some of those drums of casing-head. It would make a devil of a fire."

"I'll find a way," Cowan declared. He had not mentioned the explosive he'd brought along. "As soon as it's dark, I'll slip aboard. You and Ruanne had better go out on the point under those casuarinas. I'll meet you there. We'll have to get away fast when we go. The explosion and the flames will be sure to bring the enemy around here thicker than bees around a honeycomb."

He sat down outside the hut, as Sinker Powell had been sitting when Cowan first sighted the man. There he stayed, alternately watching and dozing while Forbes watched. It was a long day. At any moment Besi John Mataga might decide to come ashore. That was what Cowan feared most; for going aboard the ship was an anticipated danger.

There, he knew, it was one chance in a thousand. If they got him, he would be out of luck. He knew Besi John Mataga well enough to know the man had no mercy. As for Donner, if ever Steve Cowan had looked upon a face showing utter ruthlessness, it was his.

Night closed in suddenly as it does in the tropics. Cowan walked back along the shore with Captain Forbes and Ruanne. When he came to the dugout he stopped.

"Go out on the point about halfway," he said, "but stay back in the jungle out of sight. This shouldn't take me long. If I don't get back—" Cowan hesitated, gazing down at Ruanne— "you'd better go back inland to one of the villages.

"The natives are friendly if you treat them right. Then stay there until this war is over or you find a way out. But I'll be back," he declared softly.

They walked on. Cowan loaded the gear he had concealed near the dugout and shoved off.

It was deathly still. No breeze touched the face of the water, no ripple disturbed its surface. Clouds covered the sky. The heat was heavy in the humid, unmoving air. Cautiously Cowan dipped his paddle, and the dugout moved easily through the water.

It seemed a long time before he saw the dark hull of the ship. For an instant he hesitated, fearing a challenge. Then he moved on, with scarcely discernible movements of his paddle. He worked the dugout toward the stern, away from the lighted ports. Except for those two ports, the freighter was blacked out. Even as he watched, their lights flicked out too.

There was silence, heavy and thick. The dugout bumped gently against the hull. Cowan worked his way alongside with his hands, hoping for a rope line, something by which he could get aboard. There was nothing.

He picked up the coil of line he had brought, adjusted the wrapping on the hook again. Sighting at the dimness where the rail was, he threw the rope. It caught and he hauled it in, testing the line with his weight.

It was now or never. If he fell, there would be no need to shoot him. Sharks would take care of that. As if in answer to his thought, Cowan saw the streak of phosphorescence left by a big fish swimming by. He slipped the band of his carrying sling over his shoulder and went up the line, hand over hand.

He crawled through the rail and crouched there in the stillness. There was no sound, no movement. Treading on cat's feet, as though part of the night itself, he slipped forward.

Amidships—that was the place. It was most dangerous, as there would be more chance of discovery there and less opportunity of escape. But the casing-head gas was stored there. Its burning would insure practically complete destruction. And this had to be a clean job. Not one Messerschmitt was to remain. A clean job—

A sound amidships made Cowan crouch at the base of a winch. He saw a man walk out on deck, barely discernible in the darkness. The fellow stood there, looking toward the shore. Another man walked out.

"Funny Sinker ain't got a fire," one of them said. "He was always one to like light."

"Act your age, Joe," the other replied. "The Old Man wouldn't let him have one. Too dangerous."

"Chiv," Joe said suddenly, low-voiced, "you think Mataga

will give us a square cut on this money? After all, look at the chance we're takin'."

"Better forget it," Chiv whispered uneasily. "We got to string with him. I want mine, but I ain't no man to cross Besi John Mataga. You see what he done with the second mate? Cut him to pieces with his own knife. The man's a fiend!"

"Donner's worse," Joe said sullenly. "Me, I'm out for the dough. I'm gettin' mine, see? No wise guy ever crossed Joe Gotto yet. I ain't so wise to the angles in this part of the world. I'd feel better if I was in Chicago, or Memphis, or the Big Town."

Steve Cowan slipped along the starboard side of the hatch, crouching low. Amidships, he found, as he had feared, that the hatch was still covered. Working swiftly, he took out the wedges, then slid the steel batten from its place. Lifting the corner of the tarpaulin, he got hold of the end hatch cover and slid it slowly out of place, then eased it to the deck.

Swiftly he eased himself into the hole. Pulling the tarpaulin back over him, he went down the steel ladder in the utter blackness of the hold. It seemed a long time before he reached the bottom. Then he was standing on a tier of cargo.

Momentarily Cowan flashed a light. He was standing on a tier of casing-head drums, piled six high. He put the explosive down and coolly spun the tops from a dozen of the drums. Then, as he stooped to adjust the time on the explosive, his flashlight slipped and fell. The glass broke with a faint tinkle on the dunnage below.

For an instant, Cowan crouched in the darkness, his heart pounding. He dared not strike a match, for by now the air around him was filling with fumes of gasoline. For the life of him he could not recall the time for which the bomb was set!

It might be set to go off in three minutes, or five, or an hour. Possibly even a dozen hours. Steve Cowan had planned to adjust it before leaving. Now he had no idea. All that remained was to throw the switch that put the thing to work.

It might blow him up instantly. It might go off before he was out of the hatch. Or off the ship—

It was a chance he had to take. Cowan turned the button and

then straightened to his feet. He moved swiftly and his hands
found the rungs of the ladder. He went up, quickly and silently.

Pushing back the tarpaulin, he crawled out on deck. A cold
voice froze him in his tracks, with one foot under the canvas.

"So? Snooping, is it?"

The voice was Donner's, and a second later a light flashed in
Steve Cowan's eyes.

He heard a startled gasp, saw the muzzle of a gun.

"Who are you?" The voice was cold, deadly. "Tell me, or I'll
fire!"

"I'm a refugee," Cowan declared, heart pounding. "I was
trying to stow away to get out of here before the Japanese
come."

Someone came out of the passage.

"What's goin' on, Donner?" It was Mataga's voice. Then
Mataga saw Steve Cowan's face. "Well, for—"

"You know this man?" Donner's voice was deadly. "Get
inside off the deck," he snapped.

When they were in the saloon, Besi John sat on the corner of
the table. His gross, hard-bitten face was unshaven, and his
small eyes were cruel.

"So, Mr. Steve Cowan. After all these years we get together
again!"

Mataga's face flamed suddenly and animal fury gleamed redly
in his eyes.

"Again! D'you hear? And I'm top dog this time! I'll teach you
a thing or two, you dirty—"

"Take it easy." Donner's voice was even. "Who is this man?"

"Him?" Mataga's voice was ugly. "This is Steve Cowan. He's
a tramp flyer. The one I told you about who knew this place."

"Flyer, eh?" Donner looked at the Yank. "Where's your
ship?"

"Lost it at Palembang," Cowan lied glibly. "Enemy got in
too fast and bombed the field before I could get her off. Blew
off my tail assembly. I got away into the jungle and came over
to the west coast, headed for Padang or Emma Haven.

"The Japanese beat me to it, so I picked up a boat and sailed
her here to Siberut. I saw this freighter and decided to stow
away and get out."

*   *   *

Donner studied him.

"It's a good story," he said slowly. "Almost too good. But where is the girl?"

"Girl?" Cowan felt an empty sensation in his stomach. "What girl?"

"The one," Donner said coldly, "that left this hair on your shoulder!"

Deftly he picked a long golden hair from Cowan's shirt. Evidently it had been left there when he was making his way through the trees beside Ruanne.

"Blond?" Besi John's eyes were hard. "Why, there ain't a blonde within miles but that Forbes girl!"

"I think," Donner said coolly, "we had better tie this man up until we investigate a little further. I found him trying to crawl into the hatch. A minute later and he would have been out of sight."

He turned.

"Mataga, send a couple of men ashore at once. I don't like the looks of things." He hesitated. "I'll go with you."

Steve Cowan, tied to the rail on the starboard side, watched the sky grow gray. At first there had been some sounds ashore, but then the island had settled into silence.

Nothing had happened. Down in the hold amidships the time bomb ticked on. Or had it stopped? Was all his work to be futile, after all? Cowan sat against the rail, gazing blindly ahead of him, weary as he had never been. On the deck, a few yards away, Joe Gotto, the exgangster was sitting beside Chiv Laran.

Past them, Cowan could see the open manhole in the deck. He stared, then slowly his weariness fell away. He looked at Joe and Chiv thoughtfully.

"Who opened that manhole?" he demanded suddenly.

Joe glanced up lazily, shifting his rifle.

"That?" He shrugged. "Mataga. He said it would have to be cleaned. He's as bad as Forbes was. Always cleaning something."

Cowan eyed the two again.

"You don't look to me like a sucker, Joe," he said. "But your side of this deal doesn't smell so good."

"Shut up," Chiv said harshly. "We ain't turnin' you loose."

"You'd be smart if you did," Steve Cowan declared. "What's

your cut on this deal? You ever think of how much you'll get—*if* they split the dough they get for these planes? By the time each of you gets a cut, your end wouldn't buy you a ticket to a safe port. I know that Mataga. He'd doublecross his own mother."

Joe looked at the Yank thoughtfully.

"So what? If he don't collect, we can't."

"No?" Cowan glanced at Chiv, who was listening sullenly. "Why is Mataga keeping Forbes alive? Forbes has a cache of jewels aboard this ship, that's why. Did Mataga tell you that? Or Donner?"

Cowan glanced shoreward, but there was no sign of life.

"Or did they tell you there was a war on? That the Japanese had bombed Pearl Harbor?"

"Is that straight?" Gotto scowled. "Why, I'd like to—"

"What's it to you?" Chiv demanded. "The cops run you out, didn't they?"

"Sure," Joe argued. "But what the devil! If the Japanese and Nazis take the States, my racket is sunk. I can't compete with them guys. When I knock over a bank, I want to know there's some dough in it."

"I know where the jewels are," Steve Cowan said quietly, looking directly at Chiv. "We could get them and get out. Let Mataga have his crummy planes."

"Get out?" Chiv sneered. "You mean swim?"

"No, I mean in my plane. I told Mataga it crashed, but it didn't. It isn't ten miles from here. We could grab those jewels, just the three of us, and take it on the lam."

Joe studied him thoughtfully. Then he glanced sideward at Chiv, whose yellow eyes were narrowed.

"You sound like a right guy," he said. "I like the sound of it. Anyway, if the Japanese are going to use the planes against our gang, why—"

"What the deuce do you care?" Chiv snarled. "Nuts! I don't care who gets the planes. I want some dough! I'm no Yank."

"Those stones are close by," Steve Cowan hinted. "We haven't much time."

"Yeah?" Chiv sneered. "Suppose I let you loose? Then you'd get them! Don't be a sap! Mataga will be back in a little while."

"Sure." Cowan shrugged. "And then you get the dirty end of the deal. You think I'm a sap? Those stones are down in that manhole, Chiv, in a box back in the corner of the tank. That's why Mataga opened it. That's why I wanted to know.

"He's letting it air out a little, that's all. You get that box and we'll get out of here."

Joe said nothing. He glanced at Cowan curiously, shifted his rifle a little.

Chiv got up and looked shoreward. Then he approached the manhole, flashing his light down the rungs of the ladder. It wouldn't reach to the corner.

"You got that plane, sure thing?" he demanded. "Because, if you haven't—"

"You got a rod, Chiv, haven't you?" Joe cut in suddenly. "He's tied up, ain't he? If it ain't there, what do we lose? If it is, we take this guy, still tied, and head for the plane."

"How does he know we won't bump him?" Chiv asked. "We could have it all."

His yellow eyes shifted back to Cowan, and the Yank felt a cold shiver run down his spine.

"Don't forget I'm the flyer," Cowan said. "Don't forget I know where the plane is."

"All right." Chiv glanced shoreward again quickly, then he looked at Joe. "Don't let him try anything funny, see? I'll be right back up."

His light thrust in his belt, he started down the ladder.

Joe Gotto sat up a little, watching his prisoner, his eyes very bright. Cowan stared at the manhole. They both heard Chiv slip, heard the hollow thump when he hit the bottom.

Cowan tore his eyes from the manhole.

"Now it's just us, Joe. You're a Yank and so am I. Do the Japanese get this load of planes to get our boys with? You're a tough cookie, pal. So'm I. But we aren't either of us rats!"

Joe grinned suddenly.

"What was it?" he asked. "What happened to Chiv?"

He bent over Cowan and hurriedly unbound him. The Yank straightened up, stretching his cramped muscles.

"No oxygen. Those tanks are dangerous. I had an idea that in this heavy air, darned little of that gas would escape."

Cowan grabbed up the shotgun dropped by Chiv Laran and ran with Joe to the gangway. A lifeboat bobbed alongside.

"What happened to Mataga?" Joe demanded.

He was nervous, but his hands were steady. In running forward he had picked up a tommy gun from the petty officers' mess, where it had been left on the table.

"He's hunting Forbes and the girl!"

Steve Cowan sprang ashore when the boat grated on the beach. Then as Joe jumped down beside him, he shoved the lifeboat back into the water.

Turning, he led the way into the jungle, heading for the point. They had gone only a dozen steps when Cowan stopped suddenly, holding up a hand.

"Listen!" he said.

Someone was floundering through the brush, panting heavily. Joe lifted his tommy gun, his eyes narrowed.

"Hold it!" Cowan whispered.

It was Captain Forbes. The old seadog broke through the brush, his face red, his lungs heaving. His clothing was torn by brambles, and his face and hands were scratched.

"They're comin'!" he said. "Right behind!"

"Where's Ruanne?" Steve Cowan demanded.

"At the plane!" Forbes looked bad, the veins in his throat standing out, his lungs heaving. "We found it! I tried to lead them away. But they got too close!"

Someone yelled back down the shore. Cowan turned, leading the way toward the mangroves.

"Make it fast!" he whispered. "We've got a chance!"

They were almost to the amphibian before Cowan noticed that Joe had not followed. He wheeled and started back. Ruanne stopped helping her uncle in the cabin door.

"Where are you going?" she cried. "Come on!"

"Can you fly?" Cowan hesitated, the shotgun dangling. "If you can, warm that ship up. We'll be back!"

He turned and plunged back into the jungle. Even as he broke through the first wall of green, he heard the angry chatter of a tommy gun and Joe's raucous yell, then the sound of more guns. Joe cried out suddenly in pain.

Cowan burst into a small clearing just as Donner and Besi John Mataga, followed by a dozen men, came through on the opposite side. A bullet smashed by his head, and Cowan jerked up the shotgun. It roared. Donner grabbed the pit of his stomach and plunged over on his face.

Joe Gotto, down on one knee, was raking the killers with his tommy gun. Steve Cowan fired again, and the line broke and ran.

Lunging across the clearing, Cowan swept Joe Gotto to one shoulder and ran for the mangroves. Beyond, the amphibian's twin motors were roaring music in his ears.

Almost at the same instant, a plane roared by overhead. Cowan glanced up, swearing. It was a Kawasaki. It was circling for a return when Cowan boosted Joe into the cabin and then grabbed the controls.

"Strap him in!" he yelled. "Get set! I've got to fight that Japanese!"

He opened the plane wide and let her roar down the open water, throttle wide. Just short of the trees he pulled back on the stick, and the amphibian went up in a steep climb.

Roaring on over the casuarinas, Cowan gave a startled gasp. A long, slim gray destroyer was alongside the *Parawan*, and a stream of Japanese sailors and marines were running up the gangway!

Then he pulled back on the stick again just as the Kawasaki came screaming back toward him. Opening the ship wide, he fled; for the enemy was on his tail and his only safety at this low altitude lay in speed.

A roaring chatter broke out in Steve Cowan's ears. Turning his head, he saw Joe Gotto, strapped in a seat, firing his tommy gun out the port.

The burst of bullets missed, but the Japanese wavered. In that instant, Cowan skidded around in a flat turn, raking the Kawasaki with a quick burst of fire. But the soldier was no fool. Screaming around in a tight circle, he tried to reach Cowan with his twin guns in the nose, while his observer opened fire from the rear cockpit.

A bullet hole showed in the wing. Then Cowan pulled the amphibian on around and climbed steeply. Rolling over before the enemy could follow, he poured a stream of fire into the Kawasaki's ugly blunt nose.

The engine coughed, sputtered. Then Cowan banked steeply and came back with the son of Nippon dead in his sights. His guns roared. The Kawasaki burst into a roaring flame and went out of sight.

Then for the first time Cowan heard a pounding in his ears. Off to his left a puff of smoke flowered. Glancing down, he realized with a shock that the destroyer's anti-aircraft guns were opening up on him.

He pulled the stick back and shot up into the sky, reaching for all the altitude he could get. He was still climbing in tight spirals when he rolled over a little to obtain a better view.

It was like that, with Steve Cowan watching the scene below, when it happened. He had forgotten the time bomb. He had forgotten everything in the rush of action. How it had been set, he never knew. But suddenly, after these long hours, it turned loose with a tremendous detonation.

A pyramid of flame shot skyward until Cowan thought his own wings, hundreds of feet above, must be singed. The puff of the explosion struck his ship and sent it staggering down the sky. He got it righted, banked steeply and circled slowly over the roaring fire below.

The *Parawan* was gone. Where it had been was a mass of flaming wreckage. Beside it settled the Japanese destroyer, ablaze from stem to stern, with the bay around it for many yards a furnace of burning oil.

Steve Cowan leveled off and then pointed his ship south.

"Better have a look at Joe," he said to Ruanne. "He may be hit bad."

"Aw, it's nothin'," Joe protested, blushing. "Take me somewhere where I can join the Army. Boy, what I just seen! And me, I thought Brooklyn's 'Murder, Incorporated' was tough!"

AUTHOR'S NOTE
Pirates With Wings

There have always been men who went down to the sea, not those born to it, as men from the seaports, fishermen, and the like, but drifters whose restlessness led them down to the deep waters. Life at sea has never been an easy life, although conditions have improved drastically in the last fifty years. It is hard, demanding, and never without danger. It has been my good fortune to survive several very bad storms at sea, my misfortune to have encountered them at all.

Wandering men take what transportation offers itself at the moment, and wherever they arrive they drift into companionship with others of their kind. Often they become what used to be called soldiers of fortune and our now more commonly called mercenaries.

The term "mercenary" was first applied to those soldiers who fought for pay, but the money did not go to them but to their chieftain, lord, or ruler. The Hessians who fought with the British against the American colonists, for example, had their services sold to the British by their ruler.

Mercenaries are usually hired when the sons of a country are no longer willing to fight for it, so professionals are sought. And there have been professionals in every war, men who sell their skills with weapons to the highest bidder or to the cause that appeals most.

During the Middle Ages there were companies of soldiers who fought for whatever leader paid most for their services.

One of the best accounts of such a company in fiction is that by Arthur Conan Doyle, The White Company. *However, the White Company itself was not fictitious. It existed and for some time was commanded by a veteran mercenary, Sir John Hawkwood.*

The armies of the Middle Ages and of the Eastern Roman Empire were for many hundreds of years largely mercenary. In more recent years mercenaries have fought in the Latin American revolutions, for the warlords in China, and wherever someone has been willing to pay for their expert services. Often they were men who were called to serve their countries at an early age and became accustomed to warfare and the military life. Many of the old noble families of Europe were descended from mercenary soldiers.

In Ireland in the time of Queen Elizabeth there was no future for a young Irishman of family, so many sailed away to Europe to take service in one army or another. Because they flew away to far lands they were called Wild Geese. Alexander O'Reilly, who commanded the Spanish army for a time, was such a one. General McMahon who served with Napoleon was another. There were Irish soldiers in every army in Europe as well as Latin America.

For thousands of years warfare offered a young man his best chance of advancement. Due to the rigid caste system that existed in Europe the chances for an ambitious man were slight unless he went to war where courage and a strong arm might win him riches, a knighthood, or a place among the great captains of his time.

Often such soldiers moved from war to war as long as they survived, renewing old acquaintances as they moved. Yet often enough it was harder to collect the money promised as pay as to win the war, if such wars are ever won.

It was a hard world, yet few such men knew any other, and nobody mourns for a mercenary.

Nor do a mercenary expect it.

PIRATES WITH WINGS

Turk Madden heard the man in the copilot's seat roar, "Turk! Look out!" There was panic in his voice.

Turk gave one startled glance upward and then yanked back on the stick. The Grumman nosed up sharply, narrowly missing a head-on collision with a speedy ship that had come plunging out of the sun toward them.

Turk gave the amphibian the full rudder as it was about to stall, and the ship swung hard to the left and down in a wing over. Then, opening the throttle wide, he streaked for a towering mass of cumulus, dodging around it in a vertical bank.

Buck Rodd, the man in the copilot's seat, glanced at Turk, his face pale. "Was that guy bats?" he demanded. "Or was he getting smart with somebody?"

Turk kept the throttle open and streaked away for another cloud, swung around it, and then around another. He was doing some wondering himself, for the action had been so swift that he had no more than the merest glance at the fast little ship before it was gone clear out of sight. Nor did he stop ducking. He kept the Grumman headed away from the vicinity and traveled miles before he finally began to swing back on his original course.

"What's the matter?" Buck Rodd inquired. "Are you afraid that mug will find you again? He's probably scared silly right now."

"Could be," Turk Madden agreed dubiously, "but that near smashup could have been deliberate. Leone warned us to expect trouble from Petex, you know."

"You mean a guy would do a thing like that on purpose?" Buck demanded, incredulously. "Not a chance! Why, if

45

you hadn't pulled up so darned fast we would both have crashed!"

"Oh, sure!" Turk agreed. "But maybe he didn't figure our speed quite right. You want to remember, a ship that fast, diving past us that close, could cause us a lot of trouble. If he did mean it, he was probably trying to throw a bluff into us. He probably tried to scare us."

"I can't answer for you," Buck Rodd assured him grimly, "but he sure got results with me!"

Grimly, Turk Madden, fighting, roistering adventurer of the skyways, leaned forward, searching the green carpet of jungle below them for some indication of the landmarks he wanted. He was not kidding himself about his newest assignment. It was a job that gave every indication of being one of the toughest and most dangerous he had ever attempted, and his life had been one long series of tough jobs.

The vast jungle below him, known to explorers as the "green hell," amounted to more than three hundred thousand square miles of unexplored territory, a dense, trackless region of insects as large as birds, of natives who fiercely resented any encroachments on their territory, and of fevers that were as deadly as they were strange.

This was the land he had promised to survey for oil for Joe Leone's Tropical Oil Company, a job that could only be done from the air.

To make the project all the more dangerous, another outfit was in the field or soon to be there. The Petroleum Exploration Company had long been known by reputation to Turk Madden. He was himself a hard-bitten flyer who was ready to tackle anything if the price was high enough. The Petex was also ready, and they had the men to do it. The difference was that Turk possessed a hankering for the right side of the law, whereas the Petex was unhampered by any code of ethics. It promised to be a dog-eat-dog battle.

Joe Leone, the tough, fat little executive of Tropco, had warned him as to what he could expect. Leone had been weaned on a Liberty motor, had pioneered with an air circus, and had been a wing walker. From that he'd gone to an airline, and from there to the more hectic business of prospecting for oil by use of the magnetometer.

Leone and Madden talked the same language, and Joe pulled no punches in explaining.

"The first one to get a good survey of that region can get a concession. If there's oil there, we want it. An' get this, Turk. The government wants it. The Tropco is doin' the job, but Uncle Whiskers is mighty interested.

"Our country needs oil—an' plenty of it. Where does the oil come from? We ain't supplyin' our domestic needs now. An' don't kid yourself that we're goin' to make any big discoveries anymore. This country has been prospected from hell to breakfast!

"Sure! We'll find oil here an' there, but not enough. Not a drop in the bucket. That Brazilian country is liable to be the biggest thing yet, an' the folks I speak for an' the ones Petex works for are out to get that survey finished an' make a bid. So figure on trouble.

"They'll do anything—and I mean *anything*—to wreck your chance of a survey. They'll sabotage your planes. They'll kill if they come to it, don't forget that. I don't know for sure, but some of the guys behind this Petex outfit may represent another country. At any rate, they don't respect Uncle Whiskers, an' we do.

"I'd figured on you. But there was a tip from Washington, too. They said you'd be the man. Seems they liked your work during the war. So you take that ship of yours an' head for the Matto Grosso. We'll have oil spotted for you at Cuyaba, an' on the Amazon at Obido. We've got two men to send along, both good sharp boys, rough an' tumble guys."

Turk had nodded thoughtfully. "Who are they?"

"Dick London an' Phil Mora. London's your expert on the magnetometer. Knows it like a book, an' a good radio man. He's just a kid—twenty-two years old.

"You ever hear of that Boy's Ranch out near Old Tascosa? It's a setup something like Boy's Town, an' a mighty good one. Well, this Dick London came from there, an' the kids that leave that ranch are tops, take it from me. Dick had some tough breaks as a kid, but he took to the life on that ranch an' left there mighty interested in electrical science. Somebody helped him get a job at Westinghouse, an' he went from that to a job in the survey of the Bahamas.

"Phil Mora's a college man. Finished his post-grad work and went to Arabia on an oilfield job. He was there a couple of years, then back in the States, then the war. After the war he went to Syria for a year or two, and now this job."

Buck Rodd turned toward Turk. He was a big man, even heavier than Turk's two hundred pounds, and a former commercial explorer, searching the jungle for gold, diamonds, orchids, and quinine bark, among other things. With Shan Bao, Turk's long, lean Manchu mechanic, Rodd completed the party of five.

"You said something about a base on the Formosa," Buck Rodd said. "That was a new one on me. Did Leone give you the dope?"

Turk chuckled. "No, Buck, I've actually got almost nothing to go on! A few nights ago in Rio I ran into a big bruiser in a cantina, a drunken prospector with a red beard and red hair on his chest. I bought him a drink, and he told me he'd been hunting rubber and gold in Brazil all his life, so I started talking about this neck of the woods. No sooner did I mention it, though, than the bruiser clammed up. He'd been ready to talk until then, but he shut up and I couldn't get a thing out of him. However, I went back there again, and on the third night we met again and had another drink.

"Well, to cut it short, this bruiser finally comes out with a funny crack. He says, 'You look big enough to take care of yourself, an' tough enough. If you're goin' to work that country, there's a little lake in the jungle just west of the Formosa River. It would be a perfect base. But you be careful.' "

"Huh! That ain't much, is it? He say anything more?"

"Well, yes. He did say something. He squinted at me sort of funny, and said, 'If you get there, an' they take you to Chipan, tell Nato that Red said hello.' "

"Chipan? Where the devil is that? I thought that was all jungle, that no white man except maybe Fawcett, who got lost down there, had ever seen it."

"That's about right. And I never heard of any such place as Chipan," Turk admitted. "But a lake in that country? Say! That would be a base worth having, and one that would save us days of time. So where are we headed for? The Formosa!"

The amphibian droned along smoothly, its twin motors purring like contented kittens, and Turk ran his fingers through his black, coarse hair. His green eyes swept the sky, alternately searching for the plane they had seen earlier and studying the vast sweep of the jungle below them.

Fascinated, his eyes shifted from point to point over the land below. To him this had long been the most exciting country on earth because here, in one great chunk, was a great stretch of land that offered nothing but legend. Ever since the early Portuguese explorers had told their strange stories of vast ruined cities in the jungles, men, lured by memories of the Maya and Inca cities and the gold walled temples to the Sun, had searched these jungles in their minds. Few had actually penetrated their depths, and not many of the few had returned.

In 1925, Colonel Fawcett had gone into those jungles and vanished. Rumors had come out of him alive, ruling a native people. And now this story told by a drunken prospector. The mention of a strange name . . . *Chipan*. And he was to say hello to Nato. Who was Nato? Man, Woman, or God? Or was it some figment of the native imagination? Some reptile? Some monster?

Long ago, reading of this jungle, Turk had read where some Latin explorer had sighted a huge reptile, not unlike a prehistoric monster, in the Bemi swamp. And if such there were on earth, surely there could be no more likely place to find it than here, in these far green forests beyond the reach of men. No sunlight penetrated those depths below. There was hot, still heat, humidity, and the unceasing buzz of insects. At night that jungle was a hell of sound, of screams and yells and screeches.

Turk's wing tip scored the misty end of a cloud and he moved out into the vast, unclouded blue beyond, and the ship seemed lost in a droning dream between the green below and the blue above.

Then out of the green came the shaggy brown ridge of a mountain chain, and the silver of a stream. It could be the Formosa.

Phil Mora stuck his head over Buck Rodd's shoulder. "Is that it?" he asked.

Turk swung the ship in a wide circle, studying the terrain

below. "It's not the Formosa," he said at last. "My guess is that it is one of the streams west of there, closer against the mountains. Nevertheless, we'll scout around for a landing."

"Savanna over there to our northeast," Rodd offered, inclining his head in that direction. "Looks like there might be quite a bit of open country around."

"There is," Mora said. "Lots of this country through here is open. Several small mountain ranges in here, too."

Turk Madden swung the ship in a tighter circle, moving in toward the spot of open water. It looked not unlike the brief description Red had given him in the cantina, but there was no way he could be sure. He dropped lower, then cut the throttle and slid down toward the smooth dark water. Then he leveled off and, with the stick back, took the water easily and started to taxi toward the shore, keeping a sharp eye out for snags.

When they were in a small cove, Shan Bao dropped the anchor and they swung slowly, turning the nose into the wind. Turk stared around curiously.

The shore was flat and low at this point, the gravel beach giving way to tall grass, and beyond, a few scattered trees. A bit farther along, the wall of the jungle closed in, but here at the cove was timber enough for shelter and fuel, and some camouflage. Dick London was getting the boat out and Turk nodded toward shore.

"Look that bottom over as you go in. I'd like to run her up on the beach if we can. I think we might make a takeoff up there. I think we'll start flying from here tomorrow."

When they were gone, he got up and reached for his shoulder holster, buckling it in place. Then he picked up his jacket and slipped it on. Ashore, Buck was getting a fire started, and they all went to work getting their camp set up. Turk stared thoughtfully around.

"It's late, so we'll sit tight. Tomorrow we'd better have a look at things."

Dick motioned toward the spur of the mountain. "Some funny rocks up there. One of them looks almost like a tower."

Madden turned toward it. The outline was dark against the sky. It did look like a tower. He lighted his cigarette, still

staring at it, then tossed the match down and ground it into the
sand with his toe.

Chipan—what was Chipan? Staring at the strange shape
against the sky of this remote jungle, Turk Madden felt a
queer, ominous thrill go through him, a feeling that left him
uncomfortable, as though eyes were upon him. He glanced
around, and something in the manner of Phil Mora told him
the geologist was feeling it, too.

"Odd place," Mora said at last. "Gets you, somehow."

"It does that!" Buck glanced up sharply. Against the darkening sky the shape of the tower was all gone. "I wonder if that is
a tower? Or is it just a rock?"

Dick London laughed. "There's nothing of that kind in here.
This is all wild country."

Mora shrugged. "So was the jungle in Cambodia before they
found the lost city of Angkhor. You never know what you'll find
under this jungle. You couldn't even see a city from the air
unless you were hedgehopping. Not if it is really covered with
jungle."

Buck Rodd had taken over the cooking job from Shan Bao for
the evening, and Turk seated himself on a rock watching the
brawny prospector throw a meal together, and listening half
unconsciously to an argument between Mora and London as to
the relative merits of Joe Louis and Jack Dempsey.

It was not only his interest in this area of jungle that had
prompted Madden to accept so readily the challenge of this
new venture. Prospecting with the magnetometer was new,
and as always such developments intrigued him. He was aware
that the device would not entirely replace the usual surface
instruments and methods, but it would outline the areas that
deserved careful study and eliminate many others and much
waste of time.

Both Mora and London had worked with the magnetometer,
the latter a good deal. Even in civilized areas, the cost of such
a survey on the ground was nearly twenty times more expen-
sive than by air, while the difference in the time required for
the survey was enormous. The magnetometer would be towed
a hundred feet or so behind the plane in a bomblike housing,
with the plane flying from five hundred to a thousand feet in
the air, and at speeds around one hundred fifty miles per hour.

In the nose of the flying eye there was contained a small

detector element called a fluxgate, kept parallel to the magnetic field of the earth by a gyro mechanism. As the magnetic field varied in intensity with variations in the earth's crust, the changes were picked up by an alternating current imposed upon the detector. These sharp pulses in voltage were picked up, amplified, and recorded. Once recorded, these observations were sent to geophysicists and geologists who interpreted the information, with the result that possible oil structures as well as mineral bodies could be identified with fair accuracy.

Darkness closed in around the tiny camp, and overhead the stars came out, bright and close. The water of the lake lapped lazily at the amphibian's hull, and Turk leaned back against his rock and stared into the fire. Phil had picked up his guitar and was singing a Western ballad when suddenly there came a new sound.

Turk heard it first. He stiffened, then held up a hand for quiet. The lazy sound of the voice and the strings died and the fire crackled, and the water lapped with its hungry tongue. And then the sound came again, the low, throbbing sound of distant drums.

Frozen in place, they listened. Buck Rodd sat up and stared over at Turk.

"They know we're here," he said grimly. "The natives know it, anyway."

"They sound pretty far off," London hazarded.

"Maybe." Turk shrugged. "Sometimes it's hard to tell. They often sound loudest at a distance."

The drums throbbed, then died, then boomed louder still, and then the sound ended abruptly and the silence lay thick upon the jungle and savanna. Waiting, listening, they suddenly heard something else—a woman's voice singing in the distance.

The low, deep voice sang, with a strange accent. *"Home, home on the range, where the deer and the antelope play!"*

London sat up. "Oh, no!" he said. "Not that! Here in the middle of the jungle some babe starts singing cow ballads! What is this?"

"Next thing somebody will start broadcasting soap operas!" Rodd said sarcastically. "Ain't a man safe anywhere?"

Turk Madden's scowl grew deeper, and his green eyes narrowed. It didn't make sense. Not any way you looked at it.

Not even, he thought, if the Petex outfit had beaten them to it.

"You can be ready for anything," Joe Leone had said, "they've got Vincent Boling running their show, an' you know what he is. An' he's got Frank Mather, Sid Bordie, and Ben Pace working with him."

Turk knew them all. Bordie and he had tangled only a short time before, and Mather was a man who had done a short stretch in the federal pen for flying dope over the line from Mexico. The three were flying muscle men, and in this game they were playing for stakes that were enormous. And what happened back here in the jungle might never be known.

"Tomorrow we start working," Turk said, looking up suddenly. "Every man carries a gun at all times, but no shot will be fired unless you are first fired upon. If possible we must make friends with the natives, or whoever there is out here. First, remember these boys we're playing tag with are tough. Nobody is to go into the jungle alone unless it is Buck or myself, and I don't want either you, Mora, or Dick going into the jungle alone until you know your way around."

"You think we'll have trouble? Shooting trouble?" London asked.

"You bet we will. But guns aren't something to be taken lightly, and neither is shooting when you are shooting at other men. We've got a job to do, and that's the first thing. If they want war, let them start it." He grew thoughtful. "Then we'll give them all they want an' more!"

Daylight found Dick London working over his gear with Mora at his side. Turk came out from under the mosquito bar mopping the sweat from his face despite the early hour. It had been a thick, close night.

"We may get a storm," Turk said, "so let's get busy."

They ate a quick breakfast, and Turk went out with Shan to give the ship a thorough check. Buck Rodd came down to the beach and called out to them.

"You can land up here if you want," he said. "I've just been over this savanna. There's no rocks, no dead trees."

*   *   *

Madden came ashore, wiping his hands on a piece of waste. At a jerk of Rodd's head, he followed him to one side.

"Come have a look," Rodd suggested. "I didn't want the others to know about this."

The two big men walked side by side up the slight rise to the long level of the savanna. A light wind stirred the tall grass, but scarcely ruffled the heavier leaves of the jungle growth beyond. Buck stopped suddenly and pointed. In a patch of bare ground near an ant hill there was the track of a human foot—a sandal track.

"Last night," Buck said, "someone probably came down to look us over."

"Yeah," Turk agreed. He hitched up his belt and grinned. "Well, maybe we'll have trouble, but let's hope we duck it." On a sudden thought, he turned and glanced toward the spur of the mountain. If there was any tower there, he could not distinguish it now. He remarked about it.

"I noticed that, too," Buck agreed, "but if the thing is there, and it is old and weathered, we might not see it. At sundown the outline is sharper against the sky. Should I have a look?"

"No, better not. We've unloaded most of our gear here, so why don't you and Shan stick around and keep an eye on things. Sort of fix the camp up, too. Mora, Dick, and I are going upstairs now."

With the amphibian turned into the wind, Turk warmed the ship up and started down the smooth water of the lake. The speed built up, and the ship climbed on the step as he put the stick forward. Then he brought it back and the ship took off easily, skimming off over the low jungle, building up speed.

In a wide circle, he swung back toward the lake, his eyes scanning the jungle, yet there was nothing, nothing except . . . He stared again, and back in the notch of the hills he saw some taller trees. His eyes sharpened. He knew that trees growing among ruins often grew to greater height.

Over the lake, the magnetometer was slowly trailed back into position, and Mora had his camera ready to shoot the continuous strip of 35 mm film that would make an unbroken record of the flight path. At five hundred feet, the amphibian swept back over the jungle and settled down to steady flying.

Pointing the ship due north toward the far distant Amazon, Turk held the speed at one hundred fifty miles an hour.

Below them the green jungle unrolled, broken by wide savannas and occasionally by the upthrust of ancient mountain ranges. Leaning back in his seat, Turk glanced around, his eyes less on the jungle than the sky, for it was from the sky that trouble was most likely to come. Remembering the sudden dive of the mysterious plane on the preceding day, he thought of Sid Bordie, the Petex muscle man. It would be like Sid to try something like that. He was tough, but he was also a bluffer, and he always believed other men were more easily frightened than himself.

For two hours they flew north and then started back for their base, flying a route a quarter of a mile west of the first course. Turk glanced over his shoulder as they flew in toward the lake.

"Everything okay?"

"Couldn't be better!" Dick yelled in answer.

Landing the ship, Turk taxied to the shore. He saw Buck Rodd come strolling down to the beach.

"Everything quiet here," Buck said. "I didn't look around any. Mostly too busy."

On foot then, Turk walked swiftly up the slight hill through the tall grass, eager to stretch his legs. Surprisingly, the air was cool. Despite the latitude, they were fairly high here, and now, in the late afternoon, the heat was already slipping away.

He struck straight for the edge of the jungle. There was less underbrush than he had expected and, following a route that paralleled the jungle's edge, he headed toward the spur of the mountain where they had believed they had seen the tower.

As he walked, he saw no tracks, no marks of any man or woman. Yet despite the tower, if such it was, his mind was more curious about the girl's voice, singing "Home on the Range." It was absurd, of course. Had he heard the song alone, he would have been convinced he had only imagined it.

The route led up the mountainside, and soon he was out of the jungle and making his way through sparse brush and scattered boulders. Then he stopped abruptly. Before him in the path there was a track.

He knelt, studying it. The foot was moccasin- or sandal-clad, small and well shaped. The stride was even and firm, as of someone of light weight and not too tall. He had a feeling the track was not many hours, perhaps not even many minutes old.

More slowly, he walked along. Once his hand went to his shoulder holster for the reassuring grip of the gun. A flyer in the East Indies and South America before the war, and in Siberia, China, and Japan during the war, Turk was no stranger to danger, but he knew that actually, it was always new. A man never became accustomed to it.

The tracks proceeded down the path ahead of him, and then he came around a boulder and stood on the edge of the ridge, and before him was the tower. There was no doubt. It was a tower.

Turk Madden halted, stirred by a strange uneasiness. It was that peculiar feeling known to those who come first to ancient ruins. The feeling of being watched, of walking upon hallowed ground, of intruding.

It was late evening and the sun was down. The mountains had taken on the darkness of night, and the green of the jungle had turned to deep purple and black. Outlines were vague toward the lake shore, although even from here he could see the single star that marked their campfire.

Turk stood there, waiting, every sense alert, a big man, well over six feet, and his broad, powerful shoulders heavy with muscle under the woolen shirt.

The tower was black with age, worn smooth by wind and rain. It stood on a small plateau of grass among fallen stones, gloomy, ancient, alone. Yet there was a faint path down the slight incline toward its base, skirting the tower.

Turk knew that there was no known civilization here. The Inca ruins were far to the west, in Peru. The Maya ruins were far to the north, in Yucatán and Honduras, and the Mayas had never been a wandering people. There had been rumors, of course. Two Portuguese seamen in 1533 had a story to tell of vast ruined cities. A Phoenician galley had been found embedded in the mud on the banks of the Amazon. And there had been tales of a still existent Guarani civilization, somewhere in the vast interior.

Slowly, Turk moved down the path, feeling uneasy. He turned around the tower, and before him the hillside broke sharply away upon an inner valley, its steep sides scarred by broken walls and blackened stone. Here and there a wall was intact. In one place, another tower. And before him, in the tower by which he stood, was the black rectangle of an open door.

Turk Madden hesitated. There was no sound but the faint whisper of the wind. He licked his lips and turned toward the door. And then he stopped. Faintly, and far away at first, he heard the sound of a nearing plane. Then he saw the ship. It was coming low over the hills, and incredibly fast.

It could have been the same plane that had narrowly missed them on the day they arrived at the lake, or it might be another ship of the same type. Like a dark arrow it vanished over the lake and into the darkening sky beyond.

Had the pilot sighted their fire? Most likely, unless they had covered it soon enough, for such a fire was visible for many miles. Well, then, they were probably discovered now, their whereabouts known.

Yet there was still the tower. He reached into his pocket for the small flashlight he always carried and stepped up to the door.

The light revealed the inside of the tower, and before him a square stone table, polished or worn until it was smooth as glass. In the center of the table was a plantain leaf, and on it a small cup. Curious, he stepped forward. The cup contained a liquid, and when he placed a hand upon it, the cup was warm.

He hesitated. Obviously, this had been placed here for a reason. An offering to a god? But there was no image here, nothing but the smooth wall. He lifted the cup and tasted the liquid.

He recognized the drink at once. It was something similar to the sweetened *pozole* of the Mayas, a drink made from ground maize. He tasted it again, and then carefully replaced the cup on the leaf.

"Red?"

The voice was so low it sent a shiver through him, and so unexpectedly near. He stood perfectly still, goose pimples running up his spine. It was a girl's voice, and she was behind him.

"No," he tried to keep his voice calm, even. "It is not Red. I am Turk."

There was a whisper of movement, and the girl stepped into the light. She was taller than he had expected, for he was looking for someone like the Mayas, whose women were less than five feet tall, and the men only slightly taller.

She was tall, beautifully shaped, and with very large, slightly oblique eyes. She might have been called beautiful. She was certainly striking, and the garb she wore left little to the imagination.

"I am Natochi," she said softly, in the same low voice.

Nato, if you see Nato—the prospector had told him—tell her that Red said hello. Then this was Nato.

"Red told me to say 'hello,' " he said.

Suddenly, at a thought, he turned the light so that she might see his face, too. She looked at him, her eyes large, serious, intent.

"You are friend to Red?"

"Yes. You speak English?"

"Red tell me how. You will be at this place long?"

"Perhaps a week, perhaps a month. You live near here?"

He had to repeat that, and then she nodded. "Not far."

"At Chipan?" he asked, and was immediately startled by her expression. Stark horror came into her face.

"No! No! Not at Chipan! Nobody lives at Chipan, only the— how you say it—ghost?"

"It is near here?" he asked curiously. She shook her head, refusing to reply, so he took another angle. "Your people are friendly?"

She hesitated. "They are sometimes friendly, sometimes not. At first they did not like Red, and then they did. They do not like the other one now."

"The other one?" Turk frowned. "Is there another white man here? Has he just come?"

"Oh, no! He came when Red came, but he does not go away. He cannot go away now."

"What do you mean? Why can't he go?" Turk persisted.

"He has no legs. He stays here now."

Turk stared at her. What the devil was this, anyway? A white man, stuck in this country without any legs! Why hadn't Red mentioned that?

"Was he a friend of Red's?"

"Oh, no! They fight very much, at first! Many fight, with hands closed, but always he is stronger than Red. He is ver' strong, this one."

"You mean he had legs then? And not now?"

She hesitated, obviously uncertain and a little frightened. "The Old Ones, they took his legs. They cut off them."

Shocked, Madden drew back. Then he asked warily, "Why? Why did they cut them off?"

"Because he wanted to go to Chipan. Always he wanted to go. They told him he must not, the Old Ones did, but he laughed and went, so they cut off his legs to keep him from going again." She looked at Turk seriously. "It is very bad to go to Chipan. It is evil there."

Turk studied the situation thoughtfully. He wanted very much to talk to this man, to get him away from here, but also he wanted and needed the friendship of these people, for they could render his base useless if they were antagonized. More than anything now he wanted to get back to camp and to think this over.

"We are friends," he said at last. "We live at the lake. We work much. Tell your people we will not go to Chipan. Tell them we will be friends and help them if they wish it. Other men," he added, "may come who are not friends. You must be on your guard, for they may be very bad men. You must come to our camp, and see the others, so you will know them."

She smiled suddenly, and he realized with a start that she was not only striking. She was beautiful.

"I have seen them," she said. "Each one. So have others of my people. We have watched you last night, and today."

They left the tower and parted on the edge of the jungle. He turned and walked swiftly back toward the fire, which was still bright.

Buck Rodd was pacing back and forth, and when he saw Turk, relief broke over his face.

"Man!" he exclaimed. "We were getting worried! Where have you been?"

Turk accepted the cup that Shan Bao offered him and walked over and seated himself on the ground with his back to the stone.

He took a swallow of coffee, and while Shan was dishing up

the food, he explained briefly, amused by their wide-eyed interest.

"Talk about luck!" Dick said with disgust. "You walk out into the jungle and run right into something like that. A beautiful dame, and away out here, too! Why doesn't anything like that ever happen to me?"

"If it did," Phil Mora said, smiling, "you'd probably be so scared you'd still be running."

"What about this fellow with no legs, this white man?" Rodd inquired. "You think that's on the level? It's funny this Red didn't say anything about it."

Turk shrugged. "She said that he and Red fought all the time. Red must have been friendly enough with them, for apparently they let him go. I wonder what's at Chipan that this other fellow wanted so much?"

"That's easy enough!" Rodd said. "Gold, probably. What else would make a man gamble on something like that? You remember what Pizarro found in Peru? The walls of that Temple to the Sun at Cuzco were sheeted in thin plates of gold. From what you say, this Chipan must be a sacred place."

"That wasn't the impression I got," Turk said. "She seemed afraid of it. The place is tabu, that's a cinch. Evil, she said." He glanced over at Mora and London. "Don't you boys get any wild ideas. If you don't want to lose any legs, stay away from that place. And don't ask any questions!"

Yet he was less worried about Chipan and the tribesmen, whoever they were, than about the plane he had seen, for it was high time that Bordie or some of the Petex crowd showed up. Certainly any outfit that hired Vin Boling to ramrod such a deal, and men like Pace, Mather, and Bordie to carry it out, was planning on riding roughshod over any opposition. And they had moved in too easily.

Daybreak found Turk and his crew in the air again. This time they flew clear on to Obido to refuel. Surprisingly, Joe Leone was waiting for Turk when he came ashore.

"Came down to handle this gas setup myself, an' just as well I did," he said, his cigar jutting up from his tight-lipped mouth. "Boling's in town. They've got a base back in the jungle."

Turk explained quickly, telling all that had happened except about the native girl and Chipan. For some reason he was reluctant to speak of it.

Previously, he had warned Phil and Dick against any comments along that line.

"Hi, Turk!"

Madden turned at the booming voice and found himself facing Sid Bordie and a man he remembered vaguely as Vin Boling. To Boling's reputation he needed no introduction. The man had ramrodded many legal or semilegal deals in his life and was utterly ruthless, a fighter who would stop at nothing.

"Looks like you fellows were getting started," Boling said, smiling. "But you're late. We'll have this survey completed in no time. Why don't you pull out before you waste more money?"

"We'll finish it!" Leone said grimly. "And don't start anything, Boling. I know how you operate."

The big man chuckled. He was taller than Turk Madden, lithe and hard as nails. In his whites and half-boots he looked rugged enough. Bordie was equally tall, but broader and thicker.

"I want 'em to stay!" Bordie said, his eyes bright with malice. "This Madden is supposed to be good. I want to see how good."

"Want to find out now?" Turk invited. "Nobody's holding you, chum."

Bordie's face flushed dark with anger.

"Why, you—"

He swung from his hip, and it was the wrong thing to do. Turk had been rubbing his palms together, rather absently, holding them chest high. It was an excellent punching position, which was exactly why he held them there. Sid Bordie's punch started, but Turk's rock-hard left fist smashed into his teeth, and then a short right dropped to the angle of Bordie's jaw and the big flyer's knees sagged. But Turk had not stopped punching, the two blows had been thrown quicker than a wink, and the third was a left hook to the solar plexus thrown from the hip. It exploded in Bordie's stomach, and the flyer grunted and hit the dock on his knees.

His feet spread, Turk Madden looked over Bordie's back at Vin Boling. "How's about it, bud? You askin', too? Or just looking?"

Boling's eyes held Madden's with a queer, leaping light.

Turk saw the hard gleam of humor there, and something else, a sort of dark warning.

"You're rough, Madden," Boling said sarcastically, "and crude. I'm down here on a job, not swapping punches like any brawler. I'd rather like to take you down a notch, but that can wait."

As Turk turned on his heel and left, Sid Bordie got to his feet, his face pale and sick. His eyes were ugly with hatred, and a thin trickle of blood trickled from his smashed lips.

"I'll kill you for that, Madden!"

Dick London moved up alongside of Turk. "Man alive," he said. "He went down as if you'd hit him with an axe."

Leone rolled his cigar in his jaws. "Son," he said, "I'd sooner be hit with an axe." He shook his head then. "I don't like it, Turk. That's a bad outfit. I'd have felt better if Boling'd blown his top."

Turk nodded. "Yeah, he's a hard case, that one. But whatever he does will be back in the bush where nobody can see, an' if he has his way, there'll be no survivors."

Sundown found the amphibian sliding down to a landing on the lake, and Turk's eyes glinted with appreciation at what he saw. Rodd had constructed, with Shan's help, a small dock, about four feet wide and thirty feet long. Also, he had a boom made of logs tied together and anchored, forming a neat little harbor near the dock.

"We've been busy," Rodd said as they strolled from the dock toward the camp. "An' no sign of your babe in the woods. But say, I've been thinkin' a little about this Red you told me about, an' about the fellow without any legs. I know who he is."

Turk stopped. "What do you mean? Who is he then?"

"Look," Buck began, "I prospected down here before the war. Most of us in that racket knew each other. At first when you talked about this redhead you met, I didn't think much about it, but then it began to tie in. Back in forty-one there were a couple of men took off into the jungle, had some idea of hunting the Lost Gold Mine of the Martyrs. Well, when I came out of the jungle to go back to the States and the Army, it was forty-two, and they were still missing. One of those men was Red Gruber. The other one was Russ Fagin."

"Fagin? I think I know that name," Turk mused. "Wasn't he in that Gran Chaco fuss?"

"That's him. A tough character, out for all he could get and any way he could get it. If this fellow without legs is Russ Fagin, I'll bet he's meaner than ever about now."

"That's a horrible thing," Mora said, "having your legs cut off. I wonder what made them do it?"

"Nobody violates tabu," Madden replied. "He was lucky he got off that easy. Usually, they stake them out on an anthill." He studied the situation. "Shan, you can take the boys out tomorrow. I'm going over to this village wherever it is. Buck, you come with me. We'll talk to this legless gent."

As though she had been expecting them, Nato met the two men at the edge of the jungle. She stood erect, her shoulders back, her garment tight and appealing about her. Her eyes went from Buck to Turk Madden.

"You come now to visit us?" she asked.

Turk nodded assent. "And to see the man without legs," he added.

A shadow crossed her face. "Oh, yes! But please, you must not ask for him at once. My people, they are strange."

Turk looked at her thoughtfully. "You are tall, Nato. What is your tribe? You seem like one of my people."

She was pleased, he saw that at once. "My father," she said softly, "was a Chileno—how you say—Iriss and Spaniss. He was a prisoner here for a long time. He, too, tried to go to Chipan."

"Tell me," Turk asked, "what's at Chipan? Is it a city?"

"A city, yes." She would say no more than that, although after a minute, she looked around at him. "The other man, without legs, he is ver' bad man. He try to kill Red."

"Was Red your friend? Your lover?" Turk asked gently.

She looked at him, startled, then amused. "Oh, no! I was too young! Much too young! Red, he talk with my *padre*, father. He talk much with him. When he go, he say he will come back. You see, we like Red. My people all like him."

"Your mother," Turk hazarded a guess, "she was Guarani?"

For a moment, the girl did not reply, and then she said without looking at him, "You must not speak Guarani. It is tabu. Nor talk of Chipan."

They emerged from the jungle into a cluster of ordered

fields. They were *milpa* resembling those of the Maya, yet here agriculture seemed to have progressed beyond the stage of burned jungle, for the fields were scattered with leaf mold gathered from the jungle, and an effort had been made to turn the soil over.

"You plant maize? How many years here?" Turk asked curiously.

She looked at him quickly, pleased by his interest. "Maize two years," she said, "*Jican* two years."

Jican, he decided from her further explanation, was somewhat like the sweet-tasting turnip of Guatemala. There was no time for further questions, for they stood suddenly in the street of the village, a street heavily shaded by towering jungle trees, most of them the *sapodilla*.

Beneath the trees were scattered many huts, some of them facing upon a rough square. Several children were playing in the compound, and they got up and drew back into the black doorways of the palm-thatched huts. They stopped before one of the larger huts, and now a man stepped from it. He was white-haired, and although he seemed old, his body was hard and young-looking.

"Cantal," Nato said, and then indicating Madden and Rodd in turn, she said, "Madden, Rodd."

The chief spoke slowly, looking from one to the other as he spoke, and Madden could gather the gist of what he said from his gestures and expression. Also, there was something faintly familiar about the tongue, and then Turk knew what it was. It was faintly similar to the Guarani language with some words he seemed to remember from the Chamacos.

"What do we do now?" Buck asked softly. "The old boy seems friendly enough. Did you savvy that Chamaco? Seems mixed up, but I could get out a word or two."

Cantal led off, and he took them slowly about the village. It was a sightseeing tour, and Turk was interested despite his impatience to see and talk to Russ Fagin, if that was the name of the legless man. Obviously the maize crop was good, and Turk saw beans, squash, papayas, sapodilla, cacao beans, and after they had walked awhile, they stopped near another hut and were served *yerbe mate* in wooden cups.

Nato spoke suddenly to Cantal, and Turk, beginning to catch the sound of the language now and to sort out the Guarani words, understood she was asking about the man without legs. Cantal seemed to hesitate, and his face became severe. But finally the girl seemed to win him over.

Cantal turned and led them to a large hut that was set off to one side, and around it a low fence. As they passed through, a big man lurched suddenly out of the door on crutches, and as he saw them, his head jerked back as if he'd been struck.

He wore a tattered and many times patched shirt and crudely made shorts of some coarse, native cotton material. His arms and shoulders were heavy with muscle, his neck thick, and his face swarthy, unshaven. The eyes that stared from Madden to Rodd and back were hard, cruel eyes.

"Hello, Fagin," Rodd said. "You remember me? We met at Tucavaca, in the Chaco."

Fagin stared at him. "Yeah"—his voice was harsh—"sure I remember. What are you doin' here?"

"I'm with Madden here, on a little survey job."

"Madden?" Fagin smiled. "What is this, a meeting of the lost souls department? Or a reunion of the veterans of the Chaco?" His eyes held on Madden. "Well, what do you want with me? If you think I want to leave, you're wrong. I won't leave here until I kill every last one of these dirty savages." His voice was low and vicious and shook with repressed hatred. "They bobbed my legs." He chuckled grimly. "An' all because I went to their cursed Chipan!"

He hitched closer on the crutches, his eyes gleaming. "Turk, you're a man with spine. There's gold in that place. Gold, diamonds, everything. It makes Cuzco look like a piggy bank, take it from me. I got there, an' I'd of gotten away, too, if it hadn't been for that Cantal, there. He spotted me, an' when the priests got through, they'd taken my legs so I could never go back.

"Take me back there, man. I'll show you where it is." He hitched closer and the excitement made the veins swell in his head. "Listen, man." His voice boomed loudly, and Turk saw other natives coming nearer, and he suddenly wondered how much of this Natochi could grasp. "There's loot there enough for all of us. Everyone. Gold to buy the world."

"You'd better take it easy," Turk advised softly. "These natives won't like that. They'll understand."

"Understand? Them?" He sneered. "They don't savvy anything, but their pig talk." He leaned forward, thrusting his head out at them. "But you should see Chipan. What a city. It puts the Maya and the Inca to shame. An' old? Why that town's older than Rome. Older than Athens. Probably older than Babylon. You take it from me, this is something.

"You can take me," he hissed, leaning toward Turk. "To the devil with these gugus. Kill the lot of them. You've got guns. Mow 'em down. Let's get their gold an' get out of here."

Cantal touched Turk's arm, and his face was severe. He spoke quickly. Nato interpreted.

"He says we must go now," she said, her eyes were frightened. "I think he understands, as I do, and it will be bad for you."

"No," Turk said, looking at Fagin, "I won't be involved in any venture that will take me to Chipan. If it is tabu, I shall respect their tabu. If you want to get out of here, to get back to civilization, I'll take you out, some way."

Fagin glared wildly. "Fool!" he screamed. "You blithering fool! There's gold there, I tell you. *Tabu!* What do their fool tabus mean to a white man?"

Madden turned abruptly away and accompanied by the others, walked rapidly off. Behind them, Fagin raved and shouted.

"I'll get there!" he screamed. "I'll get there, an' to the devil with you all. I'll see the whole bunch of you dead. All of them an' all of you!"

Madden stopped when they were well away from Fagin and he glanced at Buck Rodd. The big prospector's face was grim.

"Crazy," Rodd said. "Crazy as a loon." He scowled. "But they seem to be takin' good care of him. I wonder why."

Turk voiced the question to Nato, and she replied quickly, "We do not like the—what do you say?—break of tabu, but we have much feeling for one touched by spirits. The priests took his legs so he could not go back, for there is much danger there, spirits that cause much sickness. But we care for him. We always shall."

"Rodd," Turk said, "there's probably something to this tabu.

Lots of white men scoff at them, but usually what a native calls evil spirits is something with a very real foundation. In New Guinea once a guy investigated a tabu and found it originated with an epidemic of smallpox. Tabu was the native method of quarantine. There's probably some good reason for this one."

"Yeah," Rodd agreed, then he looked at Turk. "I wonder if Fagin's nuts or if there is a lot of gold there. Man alive! What a find it would be!"

"Right now I'm thinking of something else," Turk admitted. He shook a cigarette from a pack and handed it to Rodd, then took one himself. "Buck, did you happen to look past him into the doorway? I did, and lying on the table, half covered by a cloth, was the torn end of a package of cigarettes. The same brand as these."

"The devil!" Rodd shoved his thumbs down in his belt and squinted his eyes. "Then he's seen somebody else recently, and if that's true, I guess we both know who."

"Sure, Boling's crowd." Turk shrugged. "This may come to a showdown mighty quick now."

Yet careful questioning of both Natochi and Cantal failed to elicit any information about white men other than Fagin. Wherever Russ Fagin had been, or whomever he had talked to, these two knew nothing about it. Yet Turk could see that his questions aroused curiosity, and before he left the village he had the promise from both Cantal and Nato that if any other white men came around, he would be notified at once.

The following week passed swiftly and without incident. The amphibian was constantly in the air, shuttling back and forth over quarter-of-a-mile intervals from the base to Obido, and the film and records piled up swiftly. Yet, as the days went by, Turk found himself growing more and more worried, and the strain was beginning to show on both Mora and London as well. Rodd took it easy. He hunted occasionally, or relieved Mora or London, who instructed him in their work. Often he prospected one of the nearby streams, or roamed the mountains with a sack and a hammer, taking samples. These trips Turk knew were more than prospecting trips, for Buck Rodd was keeping an eye on the country. He was not trusting to the natives.

On the tenth morning, Turk gestured at the stack of film, waiting in its cans to be transported to Obido.

"We'll take that in tomorrow," he suggested, "but today we knock off. I'm taking a flight over the jungle. You come along, Dick, an' the rest of you take it easy around here, but keep your eyes open."

They took off in the bright morning sunlight and headed due north as usual, but when a few miles were behind them, Turk banked the ship steeply and circled low over the jungle.

"Keep your eyes open, Dick," he said, "this is a reconnaissance flight. Boling's outfit has me worried."

With the two Pratt & Whitney motors roaring along pleasantly, Turk moved the ship down to a thousand feet and swung over the green carpet of jungle. Somewhere, not too far away, Boling would have a base camp. Twice his planes had been seen, but if they were actually conducting a survey it was not obvious, or else they were working far to the west.

That Vin Boling or one of the men with him had established secret contact with Russ Fagin seemed obvious, and if they had, they would know about Chipan. Knowing how inflammatory natives can become over violation of a tabu, Turk Madden understood that if the newcomers invaded Chipan it might mean disaster for every white man in the area.

Movement caught his eye, and he turned his head. The small plane they had seen before was just rising over the tops of the trees, and as it lifted, it turned in a wide swing toward them.

Turk yanked back on the stick and began to reach for altitude. What was coming he didn't know, but he wanted to be ready for anything. He went up in a fast climbing turn and it took him over a long savanna, the one from which the small ship had risen.

"Look!" Dick yelled. "There's some planes! Three of them!"

Vin Boling's headquarters lay before him. In air line distance it was no more than twenty miles from his own, with the native village between them. He scowled. It was odd that nothing had been seen of Boling's planes when he had been running a survey with the magnetometer.

He glanced back at the smaller plane and saw it was climbing fast and already a little above him.

"Looks like trouble!" he said, nodding quickly. "If that boy is armed, we may have plenty of it!"

London looked at him, astonished. "You don't mean they'd fight us? Like in war?"

Turk chuckled grimly. "Brother, when you tangle with that crowd it's always war. Petex knew what they were doing when they hired Boling. And Bordie, Mather, and Pace are fit running mates for him."

The small ship was a high-powered job with a terrific rate of climb, and it had passed them in the air. Suddenly, it went into a wing over and came down toward them in a screaming dive.

With one fleeting glance at the small ship, Turk opened the throttle wide and hit the straightaway, streaking off over the jungle. Yet he knew he could not hope to keep away from the smaller ship, which was much faster and more maneuverable than his own.

He saw it pull out of its dive and level off in pursuit, and he deliberately slowed. The heavens were almost cloudless, and there was little chance of escape that way. His only chance lay down below or in a sudden break that would put the ship in his sights. He cleared his guns with a burst of fire and saw Dick's startled glance. Then as the small gray ship came hurtling up on his tail, Turk did a half roll and came out of it only a few hundred feet over the jungle.

Several towering trees loomed before him, and he pointed the nose for them and put the stick forward, screaming in a long, slanting dive. He heard a yell from Dick and saw the bright spark of tracer as it leaped up alongside the cabin then fell away behind. The trees, like a solid wall, seemed rushing to meet them, and when they seemed certain to crash, he yanked back on the stick and the ship zoomed up and over. He put the stick forward and did a vertical bank with a wing tip almost touching the jungle below and turned right back on his trail, hauling back on the stick and grabbing at the space above him.

With a quick glance around as he turned, he saw the fighter had safely missed the trees, but had overshot on his unexpected turn and was pulling up now in an Immelman. Kicking the throttle open. Turk streaked away for the rising ship and let go with a burst of fire that streaked by the nose, but as the other ship was pulling out, it staggered suddenly in the air, and Turk banked sharply and swung around.

Although he had not noticed it, one of his bullets must have gone home on the other ship. Coolly, he hung above it and behind, watching the pilot fight the ship. He moved in closer, and, suddenly, the gray ship snapped out of it, pulled up sharply and, banking, swept toward Turk, guns blasting fire.

Cursing himself for a fool, Turk Madden made a flat turn, opening up on the smaller ship. But the burst was a clean miss, and the next thing he knew tracer was streaking by his plane. There was no chance to get away. The issue must be decided here. Pointing the amphibian straight at the gray ship, he opened the throttle wide.

He was hoping the pilot would take it for a suicide attempt, an effort to get him while going down himself. But whatever the pilot of the gray ship thought, he pulled up suddenly, and Turk let go with a burst that riddled his tail assembly.

The small ship fell away sharply, clearing Turk's wing tip by inches, and Madden caught a fleeting glimpse of Bordie's face, white and desperate, as the man fought the falling ship.

Madden pulled out and streaked away. Suddenly he was shaking all over and felt sick and empty inside. He glanced over at London, and Dick's face was as white as his own must have been and his eyes were round and bright. Suddenly, Turk was sweating. He wiped his face and glanced back. A puff of smoke rose suddenly from the jungle, and then a tiny spark of flame. Madden turned his head and started back for camp.

"Do you think he got out of that?" Dick asked hoarsely.

Turk shrugged. "There's no telling. When a ship crashes into the jungle like that, a man's got a chance, anyway. A mighty slim one, but I've known them to walk away. Those trees right there are mighty high, and that jungle's like a web. He didn't have much speed when he hit."

"What now?" London asked.

"Their base," Turk said grimly. "They asked for a fight, an' they can have it."

Yet when he zoomed over the savanna where Boling's planes had been, the craft were gone. However, the tents were still there, and what was obviously a storage tank. Madden turned at the end of the field and came streaking back, his twin motors wide open. He caught a fleeting glimpse of a man ducking from one of the tents, and then he cut loose with his guns and saw the tents go up in a burst of flame.

Turning, he made another pass at the field, this time pointing a finger of tracer at the storage tank, and getting it. There was an explosion and a puff of red rolling flame following a burst of black, oily smoke.

At the end of the field, Turk leveled off and headed for the horizon. It had been a hot bit of work, but a good one. He streaked away, then made a wide circle and headed back for his own base. He felt suddenly let down now that it was over, and yet he knew just how lucky he had been. If Bordie had waited him out, or hadn't pulled up when he did, it would have been only a matter of a minute or two until he would have shot down the heavier, less maneuverable amphibian. In the last analysis, in such a scrap, it was how much spine a man had, and the breaks.

Madden mopped the sweat from his face again and swung low over the lake. Then he cut the throttle and came in for a landing. The ship touched the water lightly, then took it and taxied toward the shore.

"Hey!" London leaned forward. "Where is everybody?"

Turk's brows drew together. The shore was empty.

Facing up the bank, they started for the tent, yet even before they reached it, they saw Phil Mora. The geologist and cameraman was struggling to get off the ground, his head bloody.

Turk bent over him. "Phil! What happened? Where's Rodd and Shan?"

Mora's lips struggled to shape the words, and London came running with a pan and some cloths.

"Relax, boys," London said. "Take it easy."

Madden's eyes swept the clearing. A few quick steps in each direction showed him no one in sight. If Rodd and Shan were alive, they were in the jungle. At least, he told himself with sharp relief, they were not lying here. He strode back to Mora.

"Tell me what happened," he pleaded, dropping beside the man.

"Six of them," Mora said. "They came out of the jungle when I was in the tent. Shan had gone to the spring for water. Buck was off looking around in the jungle. They slugged me when I came out."

Dick's head came up sharply. "The film! And the records!"

Turk lunged to the tent, but even before he jerked back the flap he knew what to expect. The cans and the box of records were gone. He stood then, his big hands on his hips, his eyes narrowed in thought. Suddenly all the excitement was gone and his mind was cold and ready.

They must have been close to camp, waiting for him to take off. When he was gone, they had moved in. The fight, then, had been lost. He had shot down their plane, strafed their base camp, but they had slugged Mora and got away with the film and the records. And the records and the film were the whole object of this jungle trip. If they got away with them, Tropco was defeated and Petex had won.

Slipping his Colt from its shoulder holster, Turk checked the load. Then he walked to their ammunition and slipped several extra clips in his pocket. He picked up a submachine gun and packed some ammunition down to the water. After that he helped London move Phil Mora to the tent.

"Dick," he said quietly, "you stick here with Phil. Take good care of him. If those guys come back, which isn't likely, you'll have a fight. You've got a good spot down on the shore behind those rocks. I'd move some ammo down there, and get some guns ready. If Buck or Shan come back, hold them here. We may have to get out in a hurry. I've an idea we're in for trouble from the natives, too."

"The natives?" Dick stared. "Oh, I see. You think that Boling and his crowd will go into Chipan with Fagin after that gold?"

"Knowing them, I do," Turk replied positively. "They won't miss, and that will mean the natives will go hog wild and want to wipe us all out. Better pack all our gear down to the beach and get ready for a quick move."

"What about you?" London demanded.

"Me?" Turk shrugged. "I'm going after that film and those records. An', brother, I'm bringing them back!"

He took twenty minutes for a smooth, rapid check of the ship, refueled from the small emergency supply they had on hand, and then warmed up the motors. He had only the roughest idea of a plan, but it was an idea that might work.

Not over three miles from Boling's base he had noticed another small lake. Actually, it was a treacherous-looking place, resembling a swamp more than a lake. There was every chance that there were snags, and it was very small, scarcely a patch of water among the mangroves and bamboo. However, with a bit of maneuvering he was sure he could put the ship down, and it would leave him within striking distance of his objective.

Of two objectives, in fact. The tall trees near where he had shot down Bordie's plane formed the apex of a triangle of which the other two corners were the pool for which he was headed and Boling's base camp. Also, he recalled that tall trees were often indicative of ruins and were an evidence often used as such by archeological explorers.

Turk got away into the wind and leveled off low over the jungle. The distance was short, and it was only a matter of minutes until he was circling the pool. He glanced down as he banked the ship, swallowing the sudden lump that came up in his throat.

The pool was there all right, and it was long enough, even longer than he needed, which would be a help in the takeoff.

The catch was that the pool was narrow, and there was a cross-wind.

"I'd sooner tackle an irrigation ditch!" he said with disgust.

Then he mentally crossed his fingers and, cutting the speed, came in as slowly as possible. Putting the stick to the right, he gave the ship a little left rudder, careful not to overcontrol, slipping the ship down to the right into the cross-wind. Then he flattened the ship out hurriedly and put the amphibian down with sweat beading his forehead. Taxiing as near to the mangroves as he dared, he got a line on one of them and soon had the ship moored.

Settling the .45 firmly in place, he slung the tommy gun over his shoulder and swung into the mangroves.

The earth was soggy with leaves and moss, and the jungle was filled with a strange, greenish light, as though Turk had left the plane to step into some fantastic other world where tree trunks rose into the towering green thickness of the jungle roof, their grotesquely swollen bodies wrapped in lianas and swathed in dead leaves and pulpy creepers.

Turk Madden, his dark face streaming with perspiration, pushed and struggled through the dense growth. At times he emerged into an open space where the growth was scattered along the ground, even though the roof overhead was as tightly woven as ever. Only occasionally could he get a fleeting glimpse of the sky, blue and distant.

He halted, and a butterfly with a wingspread of seven inches danced in the air before him. He stopped again as a monkey chattered briefly somewhere off in the green distance. What seemed a mottled branch of a jungle tree stirred slightly, and with the hair bristling along his scalp, Turk slipped the machete he had taken from the plane into his right hand.

It was a boa constrictor, as thick as a man's thigh. Turk stepped gingerly around the tree and moved on, avoiding the many-colored globes of the *curuju* that are filled with a caustic ash. He avoided, too, a column of ants that trailed from a tree into the depths of a green and sickly looking swamp.

Yet he made time. He found ways through the trees, using the machete but little, keeping his pace steady, and moving as swiftly as he could. When his sense of distance and timing assured him that he was approaching the savanna where Boling had his base, he moved more slowly, and purposively. Still when he finally reached the field, he almost walked into it before he caught himself. Sheathing the machete, then, he unslung the tommy gun.

"Brother," he told himself, "here goes nothing!"

The tents, now in ashes, were not far from him, but the planes had returned. There were two now, so all of the party must be present. Bordie's ship, as well as Bordie himself, was gone. That still left Boling, Frank Mather, and Pace, three tough customers, together with whoever they had to service the planes and maintain the base.

One of the ships was a big transport job, the other a small gray ship like the one Bordie had flown. It was not a fighter, but did mount a couple of machine guns.

Circling warily on the edge of the jungle, Turk searched for the men themselves.

He saw nothing, however, until finally, near a small fire, he saw a man rise and pick up a coffee pot.

"Personally"—the man's voice was strong and clear—"I wish we were out of here. This jungle gives me the creeps."

"Yeah," another voice agreed, "but if they do take that Chipan for a lot of loot, we'll be fixed for life!"

"Will we?" The first man's voice was ironic. "I ain't seen Vin Boling turning loose of anything yet. All we'll get will be what they don't want. I'd rather be out of here."

"I wonder where Sid is?"

"You needn't. When a man takes off in a ship like he had, after a ship Madden's flying, an' doesn't come back in all this time, mister, he ain't comin' back!"

"He could have gone on to Obido or Santarem."

"Sure. He could have done that, but I'll lay five to one he didn't. Sid Bordie washed out on this one. You take it from me."

There was no way to approach closer without being seen, and Turk didn't try for further concealment. He stepped out of the jungle and started walking swiftly through the grass toward the men.

"What about this Madden?" the man with the coffee pot was saying. "The way Bordie talked about him you'd think he was a combination of Jack Dempsey and Wild Bill Hickok. I only seen him oncet, an' that was the day he clipped Sid in Obido."

"Oh, he's tough, all right! Flew in the Chaco an' in China. Ran a hand-me-down airline in the East Indies before the war. He's tough, but he can be had! Like I've told Bordie, I wished I had a chance at him. Maybe I ain't no hand with my fists, but with a gun? Say!"

Turk stopped. "All right, chum. Say it!"

The coffee pot dropped with a crash, and the man's head jerked as if he'd been struck. He wheeled toward Turk, his eyes ugly.

He was a short man and stocky, with corn-colored hair in a crewcut. He had a red face and his eyes were pale blue. The other man was in a sitting position, and his face looked as if somebody had washed it in flour.

"Here it is," Turk said quietly. "I don't want you boys, but if you want to buy in, this is your chance. I want those films and the records, and nothing more. What do you say?"

The man on the ground spoke and his voice shook.

"Let him have 'em, Ed. Heck, I want to get out of this. This ain't no place for a man to die. I—"

"Shut up!" Ed snarled viciously. "You may be yella, but I'm not. Madden, you get anything here, you got to take it."

Turk's lips tightened and he felt a strange jumping in his stomach. "Chum, you get one more chance. Drop the rod an' back away with your hands up."

"Like the devil!"

With a whiplike movement of the arm, the short man drew and fired. It was fast, incredibly fast, and Turk felt the snap of the bullet as it whizzed by his ear, and then he swung up the tommy gun.

"Drop it!" he yelled.

The man laughed and steadied his hand. "Why, you—"

Turk Madden shut down on the trigger, and the gun jarred in his hand. The gun dribbled from the short man's hands and he backed up slowly, his face shocked, his eyes suddenly alive with awful realization. He staggered, then fell.

The other man might have been turned to stone. "Not me, Madden!" he gasped hoarsely. "I got a wife an' kids! I—"

"Forget it!" Turk said. "If you've got a wife and kids you're in one rotten racket. Where are those films and records?"

"In the transport," the man said eagerly. He got to his feet. "I'll get them for you."

A sudden movement startled Turk, and he wheeled, dropping into a crouch, the tommy gun ready, and then he could have whooped with joy. Two men were rushing toward him, and they were Buck Rodd and Shan Bao.

"You two! By all that's holy, if I was ever glad to see anybody!"

"We trailed them," Buck said, "we were after the films. You've got them?"

"Yeah. In the transport."

"Hell's breakin' out back there," Rodd said, panting from his run. "Vin Boling's in Chipan with Mather, Pace, and another guy. All of them have tommy guns, and they've killed a half dozen natives. Russ Fagin's with them. We hid in the jungle until they got by us. They've got Nato, too!"

"The girl?" Turk scowled. "That's a help, isn't it. If it was just them and the natives, I'd let them fight it out." He fed shells into the clip of the tommy gun. "Look," he said swiftly, "you two take the film and records and head back for our ship." Quickly, he explained. Then he looked at Shan. "You've flown that ship a lot of miles. Think you can get her out of there?"

Shan Bao listened to his explanation, then nodded.

"All right, then," Madden said, "get this stuff back to the ship, take off, and get back to our base. Load up and be ready to move out."

"What about you?" Buck protested. "If you're going to tackle that gang, I'm with you!"

"No!" Turk said decisively. "This is my own deal. You fellows get back. Shan couldn't pack all this stuff in one trip, anyway. I'm going over there in the little ship."

"How will you land?" Rodd protested.

Turk shrugged. "Maybe I won't have to. I want to get that girl away from them, and if I catch that bunch alone, I'm not going to play tag with them. Get going!"

"What about me?" the Boling man protested.

Turk turned on him. "Mister," he said, "unless you can fly that transport, or some of those guys come back, it looks to me like you've got a long walk."

On the run he headed for the small ship. A swift check, and he climbed in. It had been gassed up and was ready to go.

Evidently Boling had the same idea that he did, and after their return they had no idea of staying around.

He warmed the ship up, and then with Rodd and Shan waving goodbye, he took off. The little ship answered to the controls like something alive, and it took only a matter of minutes to let him know that he was flying a really hot job. He skimmed off over the jungle and banked around the tall trees as around a pylon.

Instantly, he saw them. Five men and a girl, one of them moving with a swinging movement as if on crutches, and behind them, some distance off yet moving steadily forward, were the natives. They clutched spears and machetes, and despite the undoubtedly superior armament of the Boling crowd, Turk knew they were in for trouble. Yet the white men had reached the tumbled rocks and ruined, vine-covered walls of Chipan.

Turning, Turk studied the situation below. The ruins of the

ancient city covered a wide area, and over most of it the jungle had moved, binding the stones together with vines and creepers. Here and there tall trees grew up from some courtyard or walled enclosure, and except for one comparatively wide space of stone terrace, the city was completely covered. This terrace, bounded by long parapets shaped like the bodies of serpents, led up to a massive pyramid. This pyramid was ascended by a wide row of steps, and, atop it, on a space a hundred square yards, was a temple, and before the temple, an altar. It was toward this place that Russ Fagin was leading Boling.

As Turk zoomed over them Boling waved an arm, evidently thinking him to be Sid Bordie, returned.

Turk skimmed out over the jungle and banked into a turn and started back. The girl was obviously their prisoner. In the hands of such men as these, there could be nothing but ill treatment and death awaiting her. No doubt she was a hostage, but knowing the fanatacism of natives when their tabu has been violated, Turk was sure that she would be of no use to Boling. Which meant she would certainly be killed. If Nato, who had helped them, was to escape, it must be by his hand.

Landing was impossible. The terrace was long enough, but it was littered with fallen stones. He looked at the jungle, swallowed.

"If there's a special god for fools," he said aloud, "I hope he's got his fingers crossed for me."

Turning the ship toward the edge of the jungle behind the pyramid, he came down in a slow glide, then he cut the motor and, with the trees close under him, brought the stick back. He came down in a stall.

There was a tearing crash, and he was hurled violently forward. The safety belt broke and he shot forward as the plane nosed down through the trees and brought up in a tangle of leaves and lianas that broke under him. He fell and then crashed into another tangle of vines. He finally hit the earth under the trees in a mass of dried leaves, blind reptiles, spiders, and decayed lianas that had hung among the tangle of vines like a great bag full of jungle rot and corruption.

All he could think of was that he was alive and unhurt. His .45 had fallen from its holster but lay only an arm's length away.

What had become of the tommy gun, he couldn't guess. He struggled to his feet, badly shaken, and moved away from the debris he had brought down with him.

The plane had hit the ground only a few feet away, but look as he might, he could not find the tommy gun.

He stared at the plane, then at the hole in the jungle.

It was a miracle, no less.

"Brother," he said grimly, "they don't do that twice, an' you've had yours."

He started away, then saw his machete lying not far from the broken wing tip. Recovering it, he started on a limping run, his head still buzzing, for the pyramid.

There was no stair on this side, and he knew that by now Vin Boling would be ascending. He started around the base, then halted, for suddenly through the vines he saw a deep notch in the side of the pyramid. It was a tangle of vines and fallen stone, but might be another entrance. It also looked like a hole fit for a lot of snakes.

Carefully, he approached the opening. Beyond the stones he could see a black opening.

Drawing a deep breath, machete in hand, he went into it.

Once inside he stood in abysmal darkness, the air close and hot, stifling with an odor of dampness and decay. Striking a match, he looked around. On the floor was the track of a jaguar, the tiger of the Amazon. There was mud here and mold. But directly before him was a steep stair. Mounting carefully, for the steps were slippery with damp, he counted twenty steps before he halted, feeling emptiness around him. He struck another match.

Torn and muddy from his fall, he stood in the entrance to a vast hall, his feeble light blazing up, lending its glow to the light that came through from somewhere high up on the pyramid's side. Upon each wall was a row of enormous disks, surfaced in gold or gold leaf, at least a dozen upon a side. Before him was an open space of stone floor and, at the end of the hall, an even more enormous disk.

Stepping forward, Turk glanced up toward the source of the light and saw it was a round opening, and no accident, for he realized at once that the rays of the morning sun would shine through that opening upon certain days, and the golden flood of light would strike upon the great golden disk, and be reflected lightly upon the rows of disks.

Awed by the silence and the vastness of the interior of the great pyramid, he walked forward, his footsteps sounding hollowly upon the stone floor, and then he turned and looked back, and almost jumped out of his skin.

A figure wearing a tall golden headdress sat upon a throne facing the disk. Despite the need for him on the surface, Turk turned and walked toward the tall dais, approached by steps, on which the figure sat. Slowly, he mounted the stair.

It was a colossal figure, much larger than he had first believed, and he could see that it would be bathed in the reflected sunlight from the great disk over the end of the hall. In the lap of the figure was a great dish, and upon it lay several gold rings, and some gems.

Suddenly, Turk heard a shot from above him, and then a yell. The sounds seemed very close, and very loud.

"Here they come!" The voice was that of Pace.

"Let 'em come!" Boling said. "Mather, behind the stone on the right. Pace, stay where you are. Don't waste any shots. Fagin, tell them unless they stop and return to their village we'll kill the girl."

Turk heard Fagin shouting, and he turned, searching for the opening through which the sound must come. And then he saw a bit of light and saw there was a stairway close behind the seated figure. From the light on the top steps, he knew it must lead to the roof.

Taking a quick step back, he picked up a handful of the gems on the dish and stuffed them into his pocket. Then he started for the doorway. But in the door he paused, for before him was a gigantic gong. It must have been ten feet across, and beside it a huge stone hammer.

Stuffing his gun back into his belt, he picked up the hammer, hefted it, and swung.

The sound was deafening. With a great, reverberating boom, the tone rang in the empty hallway. Outside, Turk heard a shout of astonishment, then a yell. Again, once, twice, three times he struck the gong, and then, dropping the stone hammer, he was up the stair in a couple of leaps.

He had hoped the surprise would give him his chance, and it did. He rushed out on a stone platform before the temple to face a group that stood astounded in their tracks, the pyramid still vibrating with the sound of the huge gong.

Nato saw him first. "Quick!" he said. "Over here!"

Boling recovered with a shout. "No you don't, Madden!" he yelled. "By the—"

He swung up his gun, and Turk snapped a shot at him that missed, and then shoved the girl toward the stair and fired again. The man behind Boling grabbed him and yelled.

"Look out!" His voice rose to a scream. "They are coming!"

The natives had started up with a surge, and Pace fired, then Mather. As their guns began to bark, Turk lunged after the girl, but Boling, more anxious to get her in hopes he could stop the natives with her, rushed after him.

Turk wheeled as Nato dodged onto the stairway, and Boling skidded to a halt.

"Out of my way, Madden! That girl can save us. Without her we're all dead. You too."

"You fool!" Turk snapped. "They wouldn't stop for her. You've violated tabu. They'd kill her, too."

"You—"

Boling's gun swung up, and Turk lashed out with his left. Boling staggered, but slashed at Turk with the gun, yelling in one breath for Nato to come back, in the other for help. Turk went under the gun and smashed a left and right to the body, and then as Boling wilted, he turned and lunged down the stairway after the fleeing girl.

A gun roared behind him, but the shot only struck the gong, and it clanged loudly, driving the natives to a greater frenzy. Grabbing Nato's hand, Turk raced across the open floor and ducked down the dark and slippery stairway toward the opening where he had come in.

Behind them, the pyramid echoed to shots and yells, and then a high-pitched scream of terror and another shot. At the edge of the jungle, they stopped and looked back. All they could see was a mass of struggling figures, but to that there could be but one end, for if the natives had reached the top of the pyramid there was no hope for Boling's crowd. One, perhaps two might get away, but more likely, none of them.

Turk caught the girl's wrist and plunged into the jungle. Her face was white and her eyes wild.

"We must hurry!" she panted. "They will come for us, too, when finished there. We have violated tabu. No living thing must go to Chipan."

"What about them?" Turk asked grimly, indicating the natives.

"They protect the tabu. That is different," Natochi protested.

Slashing at the wall of jungle, with his machete, Turk cleared a space and then moved forward into an opening. He walked swiftly, but as fast as he walked, the girl's terror and her own lithe strength was enough to keep her close behind him.

Twisting and turning, using every available opening, he dodged through the thick undergrowth. They had little time, and then the hue and cry would be raised after them, and the natives would come fast, probably much faster than he could go.

A savanna opened before them. "Can you run?" he asked.

She nodded grimly and swung into a stride even with his own. Together, man and woman, they raced across the tall grass field and into the jungle beyond. Turk's heart was pounding, and though he strained his ears, he heard no more shooting. Then, after a long time, one shot sounded, far behind them.

"If Boling was smart," he said, "he used that on himself."

Walking, running, stumbling, and pushing, they made their way through the jungle. Behind them they heard no sound, but they knew the chase was on.

What if Shan had crashed in his takeoff? What if there had been some other trouble? What if they had not found the ship? If they had met with trouble, he thought grimly, if anything had gone wrong, then it would be a last stand on the lake shore for them. And for Dick London and Phil Mora, too.

His shirt was hanging in rags, partly torn in the plane crash and partly in the jungle. His breath came in hoarse gasps, and he stopped once to brush his black hair from his eyes, staring back. He turned once more at Nato's urging and plunged into the jungle.

How long they were in covering the distance he never knew.

The jungle was a nightmare of tangling traps and spidery vines. They fought through it, heedless of snakes or swamps, thinking only of escape, and behind them, somewhere in the green and ghostly silence of the afternoon jungle, came the slim brown natives, the little brown men with their black, glistening eyes. Their tabu had been violated, and for this each man and woman must die!

A crash sounded in the jungle behind them, and Turk swung about swiftly, his gun leaping up. A native poised there with a spear, and Turk's gun belched flame. The man screamed and the spear went into the ground. Then, as others rushed forward, Turk emptied the clip into them and turned and burst through the wall of the jungle into the open savanna. Before them was the blue of the lake!

If he had had the strength, he would have whooped for joy. Even as he ran, he jerked out the used up clip and shoved in another one. The prop on the big amphibian started to turn, and with his breath stabbing like a knife, he staggered with the girl down toward the water.

Rodd and London were standing there with rifles, and suddenly they began to shoot. Pushing the girl toward the boat, Turk wheeled on Rodd.

"Get going!" he said. "They've gone crazy! Nothing will stop them!"

They shoved off in the boat, and the plane's door was open to receive them. Once aboard the plane, they pulled in the boat and Shan started the ship moving.

Gasping, Turk stared back toward the horde of natives, all of two hundred of them, gathered upon the site of their camp, stamping and waving their spears.

The twin motors talked strongly to the bright blue sky, and the big ship pulled up, circled once over the lake and leveled off toward the far blue distance where lay the Amazon.

"What about her?" Mora said, nodding toward the girl. She looked from one to the other, her eyes wide.

"She'll do better outside," Turk said quietly. "I'll see that Joe Leone stakes her, and with the job we've done, he'll be glad to. Besides," he added, feeling the hard lump of the gems and gold in his pocket, "I've got enough here, out of their own temple, to take care of her for life."

"Wait until I show her Coney Island," Dick said. "And buy her a couple of hot dogs!"

She laughed. "With mustard?"

"Hey!" Dick gasped. "What is this?"

"Red tell me much about Coney Islands," she said. "He talk always of hamburgers, hot dogs, and of beer."

Turk took over the controls and held the ship steady. He looked down at the unrolling carpet of the jungle. It was better up here. It was cleaner, brighter, freer.

They would be in Obido soon, and tomorrow they would be starting home, down the dark rolling Amazon, the greatest of all jungle rivers. And behind them, in the green solitude of the jungle, the morning sunlight would shine through a round opening and touch with all its radiance upon a great golden disk, and the reflected light would bathe in strange beauty the solitary figure of the mysterious god of Chipan.

AUTHOR'S NOTE
TAILWIND TO TIBET

Many of the great rivers of Asia have their sources in the mountains of Tibet, flowing down from the high plateaus through magnificent gorges, most of them unexplored by any European or American. How well they are known to others, whether Tibetan or Chinese, we can only guess.

It is said that many of these gorges and the grassy highlands near them have never been explored, and so it is not indicated on maps of the area where they can be found at all.

The KuenLun Mountains that border Tibet on the north are little known, perhaps not even to local tribesmen. Almost as high as the Himalayas, their peaks have lured no climbers, although many are awesome in height and obvious difficulty. Passes through these mountains are few, and some that were once in use have since been abandoned. During its brief war with India, the Red Chinese built a road leading to Ladakh and its general area over which to supply its soldiers. Most traffic has tended to choose that road and abandon the lesser passes, although yak caravans still travel some of the old routes to avoid officials and, if they can, taxes.

TAILWIND TO TIBET

The twin motors of the Grumman muttered their way through the cloud, then pulled the plane into the blue sky beyond. Below, the bare, brown backs of the mountains fell away into the canyons like folds of loose hide. The winding thread of the Yellow River which had pointed their way toward the distant hills had fallen behind. Before them lay only the unknown vastness of the KuenLun Mountains and, beyond, Tibet,

Turk Madden eased forward on the stick and slid down a thousand feet toward the black, thumblike peak on which he had laid his course. Then he banked around it and came in over the black lake.

It was there, just as he remembered it. On the far side the age-old ruins, ancient beyond belief, lay bleak and bare in the late rays of the setting sun. Turk put the ship down gently and taxied toward the crumbling structures, keeping a careful eye out for any of the stone piers that might be under the water.

Shan Bao moved up behind him as he neared the stone platform, weathered and black with age. "We'll tie her up," he told the Manchu. "I want to go ashore."

Sparrow Ryan looked over his shoulder. "Looks older than the mountains!" he exclaimed, staring at the buildings. "Who built these?"

Turk shrugged. "That, my friend, is possibly the ultimate mystery. Nobody knows anything about this part of the world. No competent archeologist has ever worked up here. I've seen Roman ruins that look juvenile compared to these."

When the ship was tied to massive iron rings on either side of the slip, they climbed out. Ryan glanced at Turk. "I'll stay put," he said, "just in case."

Madden nodded and helped lovely film actress Raemy Doone to the dock. Travis Bekart climbed out and stood looking around. There was apprehension in his eyes and a certain watchfulness that Turk didn't like. He was glad the tough little government man was staying behind to keep an eye on things.

The stone platform on which they stood was worn by long ages of wind and water, and it fronted what had once been a magnificent building, over half in ruins now. The architecture was not Chinese but something that predated even the massive monasteries of inner Tibet. The city itself, of which almost a third had been built on stone pilings over the lake, stretched halfway up the sandy hills of the valley.

At the far end of the lake the Thumb Peak pointed a finger at the sky. "I'm glad it's thumbs up!" Turk said, chuckling. "This place is gloomy!"

Their footsteps echoed hollowly on stones no white man had ever trod, and when they spoke they dropped their voices to whispers as though fearful of awakening spirits long dead.

There was no other sound. A stillness of something beyond death lay over the valley. Even the wind found no place to wail or mourn among the ruins or the hollow arches of empty windows. The platform ended in a paved street that ran along the shore behind the first row of buildings, then turned up a gloomy avenue that mounted the hill. A great stone tower had fallen into the street, which was scarcely more than an alley, making a pile of dusty rubble over which they must climb.

Shan Bao slid a long, yellow-fingered hand into the pocket of his leather jacket and drew out a pipe. Raemy glanced at him, seeing the curious expression in his eyes. "These were your people?"

"Who knows? I am a Manchu, and my people are very ancient, but this"—he waved a yellow hand—"this is more ancient. This is older than the Great Wall, older than time. It is perhaps older than the mountains."

Turk stepped to a great stone arch that opened into a vast hall, unbelievable in its height and impressive expanse. They walked inside, a tiny knot of humanity lost beneath a dome so huge as to make them stare, unbelieving.

"Who would ever dream there were such places as this!" Raemy exclaimed. "It's so strange, and so beautiful!"

"Beautiful?" Bekart stared about him distastefully. "It's gloomy as a cavern."

They walked out into the darkening street. A bat dipped toward Turk's head, and, involuntarily, he glanced up.

Beyond the rooftops and on the ridge that enclosed the valley was a small group of horsemen. They were at least a half mile away but clearly visible in the last rays of the sun.

Raemy caught Madden's arm. "Who are they?"

"Can't say," Turk murmured, scowling. "They might be Lolos. We'll get back to the ship. Bekart, you go on ahead with Miss Doone. I'll hang back with Shan Bao as they may come up on us."

"I want to see them!" Raemy protested, lifting her chin defiantly.

Turk grinned. "You'd better go, honey chile. You'd be worth fifty camels up here!"

"I'll stay," she said. "I want to see them!"

Turk barely glanced around, his eyes level and hard. "You'll go," he said, "now!"

"Let's not use that tone, Madden!" Bekart said savagely. "I'll not have it!"

Madden's eyes shifted to Bekart. "You go with her," he said coolly, "and get moving!" His eyes went back to the actress. "Take him along," he said.

Their eyes held. Horses' hoofs sounded on stone. She turned abruptly then. "We'd better go, Travis," she said. "He's right, of course!"

A dozen horsemen were riding toward them, loping nearer on their ragged, long-haired Mongolian ponies. When they were almost up to them they reined in, and their leader, a tall, fierce-looking man with greasy black hair, shouted speech strange to Madden's ears.

Shan replied. After attempting several dialects he made himself understood. "He wants to know what we do here," Shan said. "I told him we rest awhile."

"Ask him what he knows of the great mountain, Amne Machin."

Shan spoke, and the big man's face became a mask of incredulity. There was excited talk among the horsemen, then the big man spoke excitedly to Shan, shaking his head many times.

Shan looked at Turk. "He says you cannot go there. That is Ngolok country, and they are very bad men with a queen who is a wicked and evil woman. She has many slaves, some of them his own people."

"Tell him we search for a man who crashed in a plane. Ask him if he knows of any white men up this way."

After some excited talk, Shan Bao turned back to Turk. "He says once long ago a big bird landed back in the Ngolok country. He has seen it, but it is not broken. He said there was another bird, not so fat in the belly as ours, that flew near here yesterday."

"Sounds like a fighter," Madden speculated. "Who would have a fighter up here?"

Shan talked some more, and the leader got down from his pony and came forward. Squatting on his haunches he drew a rough map in the sand, pointing out the mountain peaks, then drew a line for a valley. He put his finger on one spot. "The plane is there," Shan Bao interpreted. "That line is a deep valley, and very, very rich. Caravans come from and go there from Sinkiang, Urumchi."

Turk Madden drew a flashlight from his pocket. There were several in the plane. He flashed the light on and off, then handed it to the chief. The man got to his feet to accept the gift, then bowed very low.

"He says any enemy of the Ngoloks is a friend, but he thanks you," Shan advised.

As the horsemen rode away, Turk led the way back to the ship. "We'll stay here tonight," he said. "I think the place he mentioned isn't more than sixty miles away."

Ryan was waiting for them on the dock with Bekart and Raemy.

"Miss Doone," Madden said, turning to the girl, "your trip may not be a wild goose chase. A ship like the one we're looking for came down safely about sixty miles from here."

"Turk!" Raemy's eyes flashed with joy as she caught him by the sleeves of his jacket with both her hands. "Do you mean it? Is it true?"

"Take it easy, honey!" Madden advised. "He might have

been killed in the landing, anyway. We only know what this native said, and he was never close to the ship. If he's alive and enslaved to the Ngoloks, we'll have a rough time freeing him."

"Oh, if he's only *alive!*"

Turk's eyes lifted from hers to Bekart's and he was shocked. The former Army flyer's face was dead white, the bones seeming to stand out tight and hard against the tautened skin. His eyes were narrowed and ugly.

Gently, Madden stepped away from the girl. Was Bekart so affected because the girl had grabbed him in her excitement? Or was he afraid that Captain Bob Doone might still be alive?

While the others were busy preparing for night, Ryan walked over to Turk. "What do you think of Bekart?" Madden asked him.

Sparrow Ryan kicked a stone. "Haven't got him figured," he said. "Like I told you in Hollywood before we left, the government checked him thoroughly. His war record is good. Before the war he was an advertising man, before that a number of things. He seems to like the company of wealthy women, but who doesn't?"

"Notice his face when I mentioned the plane was intact?"

"Uh-huh, I did. That hit him right where he lives, Turk, and I'm wondering why. He flew the wingman for Doone, and nobody ever knew what happened but him."

Could Bekart secretly be in the pay of the people who wanted the Pharo counter? Certainly, this improvement in the Geiger counter which had been the sole cargo of the missing plane was infinitely valuable to a number of countries.

Madden recalled Ryan's words of a few days before. "It's a new gadget. Yank flyer in India dreamed it up. He'd been working in a laboratory where they had to keep testing for radiation. The device for that's a Geiger counter. This guy dreams up a new angle on it, a much more sensitive tube, just the sort of thing that would be ideal for locating secret atomic plants. The Geiger counter will register atomic disturbances over one thousand miles away, in some cases up to two thousand miles. This Pharo counter is much more sensitive and has a directional device so they can pin down the location of the disturbance within a matter of miles.

"This guy in India," Ryan had said, "had access to the materiel and built a model, but then he was murdered. However, they put the gadget in this steel box and started it for the States over the Hump. They were flying it to Chungking, then Japan, then home. But the plane crashed."

Had that been the reason for the crash? Madden doubted it, and so did the authorities in Washington. The crash had been in the wrong place, almost impossible of access. Three times, under cover of other excuses, the Army had tried to find the plane and failed. Then when they discovered that Raemy Doone, the film star, was financing her own expedition to search for her brother, who had piloted the ship, they had slipped their man, Ryan, into the personnel for the flight. Madden's eyes searched the shadowy line of the hills, and beyond them the mighty, ice-capped peaks and shoulders of the mysterious Kuen-Luns and the towering majesty of the world's mightiest mountain, Amne Machin.

Travis Bekart was utterly ruthless. He was the sort of man who got what he wanted, regardless of price. The cold, bleak fury in his eyes a few minutes ago had not been the look of a man in love and engaged to the beauteous Raemy Doone. It had been the expression of a man thwarted who meant to do something about it. The expression, perhaps, of a murderer.

Then Turk Madden stiffened. Sparrow Ryan, who had started toward him, stopped dead still, his mouth open.

For from the distance over the hills came the mutter of a rapidly approaching plane! A drone that mounted and mounted until suddenly, with a gasp of night air, it swept by, low over the hills! It was a single-engine fighter.

"Think he saw us?" Ryan speculated apprehensively.

"No telling. We'd better figure that he did. Get out that B.A.R. That Browning's a good weapon. If he comes back and asks for it, he can get it."

The plane did not return, and at daylight Turk Madden rolled from his blankets into a crisp, chill dawn. Gathering a few sticks he built a small fire against a stone wall.

The rest of them crawled from the plane, Sparrow with a gun on his hip, and Shan Bao with his ever-present rifle. Standing it nearby he began to prepare breakfast. Turk's gun, as always, was in his shoulder holster.

Bekart's face looked drawn and worried. "Madden!" he burst

out suddenly. "I've come this far without complaint! But this is madness! Sheer, unadulterated madness! This place is ghastly, and who knows what horrors we may run into up close to that mountain? I've heard of the awful chamber of horrors in Samyas monastery in Tibet, and compared to these Ngoloks the people of Tibet are civilized! I insist we turn back!"

"How can you talk that way, Travis?" Raemy protested. "Why, would you want me to waste all I've spent? All my hopes and Madden's time? I wouldn't think of turning back!"

"I insist!" Bekart replied stiffly. "I love you and I can't have the woman I love subjected to such risks! This journey was madness in the first place! With what we know now it is worse than madness!"

"You mean," Ryan interrupted suddenly, "because we now know that Doone landed in one piece?"

Bekart's face whitened and his eyes glittered, but he did not reply, only continued his tirade. "What kind of plane was that, that flew over us last night? I know every plane that flies, and I never saw such a ship before! What would a fighter be doing here, of all places? We've been warned about these people, and every step is nearer to awful death or slavery!"

Turk Madden glanced up. "You knew all that when you came," he said coldly. "We all did. As it happens, neither you nor Miss Doone has anything to say about the further progress of this trip.

"It is true," he added, smiling at Raemy's surprised look, "that she financed this trip to find her brother. That's still our purpose, but we have another. Ryan is a government man. We're after a steel box that was Doone's cargo in the lost plane. That box is of enormous importance to our government, so let's hear no more about it. The trip continues.

"As for Bob Doone," Madden added, "if he is alive, we'll find him. If he is dead, we shall find his grave. Also"—he glanced up, his eyes bland—"I wish to examine Doone's ship to see what happened to it."

Travis Bekart's eyes sparkled dangerously. "What are you implying?" he demanded.

"I?" Turk raised astonished brows. "Why, nothing! Only that's the usual course when a crashed plane is found. We must find the cause of accidents to prevent future trouble. What else would I imply?"

Raemy Doone stared searchingly at Bekart, and there was a cold and curious light in her eyes. Raemy, Turk decided, was an astute young woman.

Dark water rolled back from the ship. Turk gunned the amphibian and it lifted, the water of the black lake dropping away below. He came back slowly on the stick, skimming over the ridge and lifting the ship toward the gray clouds. In the distance, its mighty granite shoulders lost in crowding gray cumulus, was the icy mass of Amne Machin, the mountain that was a god.

Turk glanced at the altimeter. "I'm going up," he said. "We'll just have a look." They adjusted their oxygen masks and climbed. Clouds came and fell away. They skimmed an ugly ridge, soared past a glacier created peak, and climbed on. The towering peak of Amne Machin still hung over them.

"Going on up?" Ryan gestured with his thumb.

Madden shook his head affirmatively. Later, when they had descended to a lower level again, he glanced over at Ryan. "Want my guess? I'd say that peak wasn't an inch under thirty-one thousand feet, about two thousand higher than Mount Everest! Joe Rock, one of the two white men who ever got within as near as seventy-five miles, estimated it to be over twenty-eight thousand, but he was conservative. Some of the war flyers figured it to be over thirty-three thousand!"

"Gives me chills to look at it!" Ryan said. "Now where's this plane we're lookin' for?"

"On a plateau. We should be there in a few minutes." The Grumman slid down through scattered clouds and skimmed over a dark forest. Far below them something dark moved on the stone-covered field and vanished under the trees with a queer, bobbing run.

"What was *that*?" Raemy demanded, over Madden's shoulder.

He shrugged. "Nothing I ever saw before. There are rumors of queer animals we've never seen!"

"You mean that no white man ever saw?" Raemy was incredulous. "Not even in Hollywood?"

"We're not speaking of varieties of wolves," Turk said coldly. "But only in the last few months they have been finding animals in the Congo no white man had ever seen. A new type of rhino, a wild boar as big as a bull. Who knows what they'll find up here."

She gestured at the country below. "How much of this is unknown country?"

Madden shrugged. "Probably a chunk as big as Arizona. Tibet itself is just a shade less than the combined areas of Arizona, California, and Nevada. The population is estimated to be about the same as California's."

"Look, Turk!" Ryan exclaimed. "There's the plane!"

"*Stop!*" The voice was cold and deadly calm. "Fly back to the lake where we stopped last night, and start right now!"

Rigid, Turk Madden looked up. Travis Bekart, a .45 Colt in his hand, was crouching behind them. "Put this ship down," he said, "and I'll kill you!"

Madden's eyes were quiet, calculating swiftly. His quick glance had assured him that Bekart had slipped into a chute harness. If he shot, he would bail out immediately.

"Why, sure!" Turk said. "If you feel that way!" Then, instantly, he snapped into a vertical bank. Hurled from his position, Bekart's head slammed into the corner of a seat and he collapsed.

Turk glanced at him and watched Shan take the gun from the fellow's hand, then bind them securely. Raemy watched, her eyes wide and strange.

"What got into him?" Sparrow asked, speaking to nobody in particular.

"I think," Turk said as he skimmed back over the plane below, "that he would rather we didn't see this ship! It makes me kind of curious!"

He banked slightly and studied the plateau thoughtfully. "What do you think, Ryan?"

"I think she looks okay. Put her down. After all, Columbus took a chance!"

"Cross your fingers then!" Turk swung around into the wind and came in for a landing. He knew he wasn't going to like it, but here they were.

As they swooped down, Ryan suddenly touched him on the shoulder. "Pick her up," he said, "there's a lake in that hollow!"

Turk shot past the plateau and circled wide over the valley. Sparrow was right. There was another black lake, almost identical with the one seen previously, and here, too, there were ruined buildings, but here they surrounded the lake on three sides. The lake was scarcely more than a mile from the plane on the plateau.

Turk Madden slid down toward the lake, leveled off, and came in fast, skimming the water lightly. He brushed the low waves, brushed them lightly again, and then the ship took the water smoothly and he taxied in toward another lonely, lost, and ruined town.

"This country," Ryan said, "must have been quite a place at one time!"

Madden nodded. "Hear about that pyramid they found in Shensi? Over fifteen hundred feet high. The biggest one in Egypt is only a third of that height, and about a third of the base line. Nobody knows anything about it. Hell, they'll find there was civilization in China six thousand years ago before they are through!

"There's been almost no excavation there, and none in Shensi. All we know of Chinese civilization is what we can see and read, and that's old enough. Somebody should do some excavating in Central Asia, and in extreme western China.

"Nobody knows much about Tibet above ground, or Sinkiang, or Turkestan, so how can they figure on the ancient history?"

When the ship was anchored, Turk got out on a pier and took a rifle with him. "I'll take Shan Bao and Miss Doone," he said. "Stick with the ship, Sparrow. Later, we'll leave Shan an' you an' me will have a look see. Okay?"

Ryan nodded. Bekart was coming out of it. "Lie still, sweetheart," Ryan said, "or that slap you got on the noggin will seem like a love tap." He looked up at Turk. "Think I'll interrogate this guy. Maybe he'll talk."

"Better wait until we see this ship," Madden advised. "I've got an idea."

He paused when they reached the shore. Rows of ancient buildings of time-blackened stones lined the water's edge. Here, too, some of them were built on stone pilings over the water, evidently as a means of defense. But the city had outgrown what was evidently merely a beginning and had gone ashore, and crawled slowly around the lake. Two mountain streams flowed into the lake, which had only a very narrow visible outlet to the south.

The sky was gray and unbroken by any rift in the clouds. The air was damp, and there was a faint, musty smell. Their footsteps echoed hollowly so Turk was glad when they emerged from the age-blackened walls and started up the scarred slope of the hill.

The bomber lay on its belly some fifty yards away, a dark spot on the white snow. No landing gear was down, but wings and prop were intact. Turk glanced at Raemy. "I'd better look first," he suggested.

Her eyes flickered, frightened. "Please. Would you?"

His feet crunched on the thin snow. Here and there the wind had revealed the black rock and gravel surface of the plateau. No vegetation could be seen. The ship looked lost and alone, and his heart began to pound as he drew near. He turned as his hand touched the door and glanced back.

Raemy stood on the snow, a silent, lonely figure. She was tall and stood well up to him when they were together, but now she looked forlorn and very small. "Look!" Shan pointed.

Turk's eyes followed the gloved finger. The cowl of the nearest engine was bullet-riddled. He felt his scalp tighten, and his eyes swept the fallen ship. Left motor shot out, tail assembly shot to shreds. The guy had performed a minor miracle to get down in one piece.

He pulled the door open. It came so easily he almost lost his balance. He peered within. It was dark and empty, with the chill of something long lifeless.

It had been looted of everything portable. If the crew had been alive when they landed, they were gone now. Perhaps to death or captivity. The steel box was missing, and there were dark stains on the instrument panel, the altimeter smashed by a bullet.

Raemy was walking toward the ship. Madden shook his head at her. "No sign of anybody, but the ship was shot down."

"*Shot* down?" Her eyes questioned him. "By the Japanese?"

"There were no Japanese in this area. It must have been someone else."

Her face looked old and tired. She kicked her toe into the crusted snow. "Travis?" she asked. "He flew as fighter escort—"

"Who knows? He acted strange, but it could be something else."

"Are . . . any of them—"

"No." He took her by the arm. "Want to look? I think the copilot was hurt. There's some blood."

Shan Bao muttered, and Turk turned. Shan was pointing at a crude cairn of stones. Raemy stumbled toward it, and they followed. Turk's face was somber, yet when he saw the name he felt a wave of relief go over him. Scratched crudely on a stone slab atop the cairn were the words:

WILLIAM A. LYTE, LIEUT., A.A.F.
Killed October 9, 19

The date was incomplete. "Interrupted," Turk said, "by somebody, or something. Lyte was the copilot."

"I should be sorry," Raemy said, "but somehow I can only be glad it isn't Bob."

When they returned to the lake Ryan was waiting. "Found a building that's intact," he said, "a good hideout."

"We'll make this our base," Madden said, "from here on we work on the ground all we can. Save gas and attract less attention. Shan can remain with the ship. We'll go, Ryan."

"And I," Raemy told him.

Madden hesitated. Then he shrugged, smiling at her. "All right, but you're inviting the risk and will have to take the consequences. From here on it will be very dangerous."

"I know."

She spoke quietly and seriously, and Turk looked at her again and was convinced. Ryan walked back inside, and Raemy stood there beside Madden, staring out over the lake.

"Madden," she asked suddenly, "how do you suppose he was shot down?"

Turk hesitated. "There's no answer to that. We've seen one or maybe more planes. Bekart said he couldn't identify the one he saw. Well, I couldn't either. They may have shot your brother down."

Raemy looked at him. "If you think anything else, tell me."

"It's only a hunch, and I've no motive to ascribe."

"You mean Travis?" She looked at Turk seriously.

"Well, it does seem strange, I think, that he should do everything to keep us from landing. Almost as if he knew what we would find."

"Yes, I thought of that. But why would he do it?"

That made Turk hesitate. Raemy and her brother were both wealthy. With Bob Doone dead, all the wealth was hers. Then, if she should marry, and if after awhile she died . . .

"I've no idea," Turk replied.

Dawn found them, each carrying a rucksack and rifle, heading down the vague and ancient trail that led through the ruined city. Turk walked in the lead, followed by Raemy. Behind her was Sparrow Ryan.

The light was cold and gray, and the path mounted, skirting the side of the mountain, weaving along through canyons and up steep mountainsides. With every mile the way became steeper and the terrain more rugged. Once they heard a plane and hid, waiting until the sound died away. It was below the clouds from the sound, but it did not fly over them.

Ahead of them the canyon ended suddenly in a wide pool enclosed by a grove of willows and poplar. Beyond the grove green grass waved in a wide field!

They halted under the trees. Before them lay a long and very deep canyon at the end of which loomed the massive towers of an ancient monastery, or what appeared to be such. Nearby, several men worked over an irrigation ditch.

The monastery occupied the whole end of the valley, and buildings were constructed halfway up the steep sides at that end. Suddenly a man on horseback rode from the trees on the far side and neared the workers. He shouted angrily at one, and as the man straightened to reply the horseman felled him with a blow from the butt of a whip.

"Rough, isn't he?" Ryan whispered. "I'd like to—"

"Wait! One of the men is coming this way!"

One of the workmen, carrying a crude wooden shovel, walked slowly toward them. Turk's eyes narrowed. "A white man! If that's your brother," he whispered to Raemy, "don't run out there! Everything depends on care now!"

The man plodded to a sluice gate and lifted it to let water into a ditch. As he leaned over, Turk spoke. "Don't look up. If you know English, nod your head!"

The man jerked as if shot at the sound of Turk's voice. He rested his hands on the gate, then he nodded.

"Are you from the American plane on the plateau?"

"Russky," he said. His voice carried over the few yards of water. "Nine Yanks here. Three from that plane."

Raemy repressed a gasp and Turk's grip shut down hard on her arm. "You are prisoners?"

"Slaves. There are many of us. Most are Chinese. Can you help us?"

"Yes, but be careful! You work here every day?"

"Today and tomorrow. After tomorrow in a valley six miles east. There will be thirty white men."

The horseman had turned and was watching the man at the gate. "Don't take chances. Is the American named Doone with you?"

"Young is here. Doone is at the Domed House. I will see him tonight in prison."

"Tell him we have come for him. Tell him we'll find a way to help. Can we talk to one in command here?"

"No!" he said violently. "That would be fatal! She is a fiend!"

The horseman had started toward them, but was still some way off. "What are the planes?"

"There are five of them, three fighters and two transports. Be careful, I go." The man closed the gate and shouldered his shovel.

Turk drew back and they retreated into the canyon. "You heard," he said briefly. "Your brother's alive. We've no idea what shape he's in. If they've a valley like that, with so many slaves, they must have a considerable force themselves."

"But planes?" Ryan protested. "This is fantastic!"

"Why? Some of them undoubtedly learned to fly with the Chinese. Some of the flyers might be Chinese who joined them."

"How could anyone dream of such a place?" Raemy exclaimed.

"We've known for years," Turk said, "that Tibet had monasteries full of warlike monks. We've known that the Lolo tribesmen kept slaves, and not long ago the Army sent men among them to search for American flyers. But if any were held as slaves you can be sure they were well hidden before the Army men got there! These Ngoloks are infinitely worse than the Lolos!"

Shan Bao met them at the landing. He spoke to Madden in Mandarin.

"You take it easy," Turk said. "Shan wants to show me something."

Shan led the way to a temple built partly over the water. Part of the wall on the lakeward side was missing, and inside almost half the space was water. Evidently from the iron rings, boats had once been kept there. It was a perfect hangar for the amphibian, even to a ramp leading into the water.

When the ship was concealed, Turk turned to Ryan. "Tomorrow you and I hit that valley!" He glanced at Raemy. "This time you stay here. Some of this won't be pretty to watch!"

She started to protest, but when her eyes locked with his she was still. In the morning when the two started off at daybreak, she looked at him. "Be careful, won't you?"

"Of Bob? Don't worry, he'll be all right."

"I mean you!" she said, her chin lifting.

Turk looked around at her and she flushed. "Yeah," he said, "I'll be careful!"

For an hour they watched the valley. Thirty-two prisoners worked there, guarded by seven men. All were armed, four of them with rifles.

"The first one will be that guard in the green coat," Turk said. "I'll take him."

The guard was a big man, and he looked rugged. He moved toward the edge of the brush, and like a wraith, Turk rose behind him. He struck the guard on the small of the back with his right fist, shooting the midsection of his body forward as his left forearm slid across the guard's throat. Off balance by the blow to the base of the spine, the guard was pulled back sharply. Then Turk's right arm slipped under the guard's right armpit and his hand clasped the back of the guard's head. With his left hand Turk grabbed his own right forearm. Then he jerked back with his left forearm and pushed with his right hand.

The guard struggled, kicked, and tried to claw madly at Turk's iron grip, but the pressure on his windpipe was too great. Turk held the pressure for a full minute while Ryan watched the other guards.

The nearest worker had noticed but continued with his labors. Then he moved toward them. "Good show, Yank!" he said. "We're all primed and ready!" He picked up the fallen man's rifle, and extracted the ugly knife from the guard's waistband.

Quickly, he donned the green coat and coolie hat, then started along the line of workmen, whispering in a low voice. One of the other guards sauntered toward him, and as he neared, the Australian wheeled suddenly and slashed with the knife. The guard fell, blood gushing from his slit throat.

The Aussie gave a low whistle, and like a cloud the prisoners wheeled and closed over the remaining guards. The man on the horse who had been riding toward Turk's waiting place grabbed at his pistol, but Ryan darted from his hiding place and leaped astride of the horse behind him. Together they tumbled from the horse, Ryan on top. He chopped viciously with the barrel of his own pistol, then again.

Ryan got up, wiping sweat from his face. He walked toward the guard Madden had jumped. He glanced at the guard, then up at Madden. "You're thorough!" he said grimly.

The prisoners crowded around. A tall blond man pushed forward. "I'm Young," he said. "I was in the ship with Doone. They've got him up in the Domed House, questioning him about our cargo. Some strange white man came to the Domed House a while back, and ever since then they've been in a dither."

"We'll get out of here fast. Those with the rifles fall behind for a rear guard. Ryan, you lead off."

Young, who had the pistol from the fallen horseman, walked beside Madden. "God, man!" he said. "You can't guess what it meant to us when we heard you were here. Kalinov told us last night." Young glanced at Turk. "That cargo of ours seems to excite a lot of people!"

"Ryan's here for that reason," Turk said. "I've my instructions, too. We've got to get that steel box for our government."

Young shrugged. "Doone's the only one knows where it is."

"Give me the dope," Madden suggested. "What can we expect?"

"There's at least three thousand men in this monastery. Probably around three hundred modern rifles including twenty or thirty Tokarev semi-automatic rifles. It's as good a gun as our Garand. Also, they have some Degtyarov light machine guns, all stolen or smuggled out of Russia by agents of these people. The Domed House, which you can identify by shape, is the heart of the place. I've told you about the planes. The pilots are Ngoloks.

"They have two flying fields and a couple of emergency fields with a fighter plane located at each. They've a leader with brains named Bo Hau. He's been to China and India and has an education of a sort. Tall, big-shouldered fellow."

No part of the situation looked good. Only a few of the escaped men were armed, and there was little food available. They could expect determined pursuit within a few hours. Turk fell in beside Ryan. "You stick by the ship with the man with the pistol, I'll take the four men with rifles."

"Why not take the plane and knock off one of those emergency fields? Then we'd have rifles and ammunition?"

"And run into a fighter? With this ship of mine? A pursuit ship would fly circles around me! Unless we hit 'em before they got off the ground. Strafe the field—but it would be taking an awful chance!"

"The whole thing is a gamble," Ryan said. "Don't worry about Raemy! That gal has nerve!"

Turk turned to a huge red-bearded Scotsman. "You know where the emergency fields are located?"

"Helped build them! One's about nine miles east in the mountains. Concealed, but impossible to use in bad weather."

"How long to get to it on foot?"

"Three or four hours, if we're lucky. It's pretty rough going."

"All right," Madden told them. "I'll keep Young with me. You," he told the Scotsman, "will lead this party. I'll give you four hours. Your job is to keep that fighter on the ground. Don't damage it if you can help it, and shoot anybody who tries to get it off the ground."

*   *   *

Young watched the rescued prisoners as they turned off into a canyon leading to the mountains. "They've got a mighty slim chance!" he said.

Turk nodded. "So have we all. Four men with rifles can make life miserable around any landing field. Knowing the country they have a good chance of getting away with it. The Ngoloks won't expect them to head that way." He turned toward Young. "We have one prisoner, your former escort pilot!"

Young's face went cold. "He shot us down! Never gave us a chance!"

"Why?"

"We never figured that out," Young admitted. "He'd been very friendly to Doone."

"Doone ever mention that Bekart had met his sister?"

"Come to think of it, Bekart was with him on leave once."

"With Bob dead, she'd inherit everything. That may have been it. He could go back, be the sympathetic friend, marry the gal, and then—"

"Ugly mess!" Young stared at the peaks. "Lyte was shot right through the chest. Three-fifties!"

There was no sign of Shan Bao as they drew near the ruined city. Nor any other sign of life and movement. Fear mounting like a tide in his throat, Turk started forward when Shan burst from a building. "He's gone! I go to hunt for wood, and he got away!"

Turk grabbed Shan's arm. "Raemy?"

"She gone, too! Also, her gun!"

Turk rushed to the plane. So far as he could see, nothing was disturbed. "Go over it, Shan! Quick!"

He looked at Sparrow. "We'd better have a look. Maybe we can catch them before they've gone far."

"No use!" Shan Bao protested. "They gone maybe two hours!"

Turk Madden's face was cold and ugly. Despite Shan's protest, he turned and, helped by Young and Ryan, made a careful survey of all the ruined buildings. There was no sign of life, nor could any tracks be found on the pavement or hard ground.

He had failed thus far to free Bob Doone. The steel box was still in the hands of the Ngoloks, or hidden somewhere. And now Raemy had been taken from him.

When they returned from their trek, Shan was awaiting them. "Ever't'ing okay," he said. "Ever't'ing good."

Madden checked his watch. An hour to go before they took off. Ryan dug into the food and got out some crackers and cheese while Shan made coffee. In silence, the four men ate.

Turk got up finally and walked outside. He looked big and grim in his worn leather jacket, his head bared to the chill wind, his eyes hard as they studied the gray, barren sky. He turned and came back in, checking his .45 grimly.

"Warm her up, Shan, we'll start now!" He looked around again, then glanced at Young. "Better have a look outside. Watch until I call you. If one of those fighters shows up, we're sunk!"

Minutes later he called Young, then followed Ryan into the ship, they taxied out on the lake, and he revved her up and then started her down the dark water. The motors roared beautifully, and he gave her plenty of time for the air was cold and light. As he eased back on the stick she lifted gently, slapped a wave, and lifted toward the rocky crest of one of the hills skirting the lake.

Turk shot straight away from the lake, climbing steadily. At five thousand he swung in a wide curve and headed back. Then he lifted higher, and higher. Far below and off to his left he could see a tip of the green valley. Young waved him further to the right and he banked the ship and headed for a tall, ice-capped spire of black rock almost due west.

Suddenly, he saw the field. It was on a small plateau, and at one end there was a stone hangar and a smaller building nearby. As he pushed forward on the stick and shot down toward the field he saw men burst from the smaller building and one of them rushed toward the hangar, others lifted rifles and although they must have been firing, he heard no sound of the shooting.

The man running toward the hangar suddenly stumbled and fell headlong and lay there, a dark spot on the pavement near his head. Then Turk opened up and the harsh yammer of his own guns blotted out sound and he saw men fold and go down as if blown by a powerful wind.

He dove toward the smaller building and the men with rifles and saw men scatter in every direction, and then he was over the building and zooming up to swing back over the field. Men had scattered into the brush, but he came down fast and let go with another burst at the smaller building.

When he came around for another pass he saw men running out on the plateau waving their arms at him. He skimmed by overhead, then swung around and came in for a landing.

As he got out, he saw men pouring into the smaller building and coming out with rifles. Scotty met him, a broad grin on his face. "We got nine of them, all told. One man got away, but several of ours are after him."

"How about weapons?" Turk demanded quickly.

Young had started on a trot for the hangar.

"There's twelve more rifles," Scotty said, "as nearly as we could figure. We'll know in a minute."

Turk walked toward the hangar after Young. In a few minutes they had the news. Of the thirty men they had in all, aside from his own crew, sixteen of them now had rifles and eight more had pistols. The others had found old iron swords and one a pike.

Turk walked into the hangar, and Young was standing there looking at the ship. Young nodded at it. "Ever see anything like *that*?" he demanded.

"Yeah," Turk walked around it thoughtfully. "Looks like an improved version of a Russian ship they had in Spain during the Civil War. Some of the Russians who fought with the Loyalists flew them."

"The other ship's the one we should have," Young said. "I think it's a P-40. One stolen from the Chinese, probably."

Scotty came in with the escaped prisoner. He was a rugged, hardy-looking gent. "What happens now?" Scotty demanded.

"We get out of here," Turk said, "and quick. We've got a lot to do. At least, Ryan and I have. And we're taking this ship!"

Young's brow furrowed. "I fly a little, but I never tackled anything that looked that hot!"

Madden shrugged. "I'll fly it. Shan Bao knows my ship. You can go back to the lake with him. He could take four or five of you."

"We'll march it," Scotty said, "all of us!" He grinned at Turk. "We might run into a bunch of those 'Loks, and the boys are spoilin' for a fight!"

Turk checked the ship himself. There was plenty of gas, and he found a buried tank near the hangar that was almost full. He yelled at Shan, and the Manchu refueled the Grumman.

When they had gone, he walked outside. The ship had been wheeled out before they left, and he had taken a few minutes to look around. He hadn't wanted to tell them, but he knew what he was going to do. He was going hunting for that other pursuit ship. From what he knew of the fighter he had, he knew she was a plenty hot ship. Also, he was going to teach them a lesson or two. They had it coming.

He walked outside and got into the fighter. He warmed her up. She was a two-motored job, bearing a resemblance to the Russian pursuits he had seen in Spain. What did they call them? He scowled, trying to remember. Masca—Mosca, something like that.

The motors purred evenly and smoothly. Carefully, he opened her up a little, and the ship trembled with the burst of added power. Turk passed his tongue over his lips. "Here goes everything!" he said softly, and, his eyes widened a little, he started the ship down the plateau.

It gathered speed and he opened the throttle wider. The black cliffs faded in a roar of thundering speed. He felt the lift of the ship as it reached for the air and he came back on the stick and felt the earth fall away beneath him. He eased back further, and the little fighter began to climb.

His eyes were bright. "Whoever built this baby," he said, "knew what he was doing."

Roaring with power the ship shot skyward like an angry hawk, and deftly he put her through her paces. She had it—speed, power, maneuverability. He swung her around, and headed between two gigantic peaks and darted through to see the green valley far, far below him, and even as he glimpsed it, he saw the Grumman far away to the east and north, and sweeping down toward it was the other pursuit ship!

Turk banked his fighter steeply and whipped around to dart after the other ship like a sparrow hawk after a hen! His twin motors roaring, his heart singing with the lust for battle, he cleared his guns with a burst and then swept down on the other fighter.

It was no P-40 or anything like it, but almost a duplicate of his own ship, and some sixth sense must have warned the pilot, for he suddenly pulled up sharply and swung around, wondering at the actions of his companion fighter. Turk cured him of his wonder in a quick burst as the fighter swung past his guns. It was ineffective, to all appearances, except to warn the enemy fighter that he was in for trouble.

The other ship made a flat turn and started for him, but flying fighters was an old story to Turk Madden. He had flown almost every kind of ship in the air. Yet the enemy pilot had been trained well, and he handled his ship like it was part of him.

"Okay, Bud," Turk said, "you want to play!" He gave the ship everything she had and started for the other fighter, head on. For what seemed minutes they rushed down at each other, yet Turk knew it was only a fleeting instant, then, suddenly, the other pilot broke and hauled back on the stick. The nose of the plane went up, and he went up and over in a wild, desperate effort to escape what seemed fiery and certain death in a head-on collision. And in the fleeting instant when his underside was exposed, Madden poured a darting stream of fire into the other ship!

He banked steeply and swung away, then circled and started back, but the enemy fighter, smoke pouring from it, was headed for the mountains, far below. Even as he watched, the smoke turned to a sudden, crimson burst of flame—and then where the ship had been there was only a puff of smoke and a few disintegrating fragments.

A hand fumbled for his brow and he wiped away the sweat. Then he headed down and south for the lake. He would be able to land beside Doone's wrecked transport. The plateau was long enough, and from what he knew of it from his visit to the wrecked ship, it was good enough for a landing. Getting off again might be quite a problem. If he ever tried.

The Goose was down on the lake when he circled over and dipped his wings, then he darted away, headed into the wind, and eased the fighter to a landing on the plateau, taxiing to a place close beside the transport.

Scotty and Young were there to greet him as he started down the hills. "Get him?" Young demanded eagerly.

"Yeah." Turk mopped his brow and grinned at them. "I hope there's no more of them!"

He glanced from one to the other. "Either of you ever been in that Domed House?"

"I have," Young said. "Don't know much about it, though."

"I'm going in there," Madden said. "I've a hunch that's where Bekart went and where he took Raemy. We've got to get her back, get Doone, and get that steel box. And it's got to be done fast, commando stuff."

"You can count me in," Scotty said.

Madden shook his head. "No. I'll take Shan Bao because he talks this stuff a little. I'll take Ryan because he's small, tough, and it's his job, anyway. And Young here because he knows something about it, about the Domed House, I mean."

When the last straggler had come in and the rescued prisoners were gathered around, eating and drinking coffee, Turk Madden began going through them, one by one. Each man talked, through interpreters when necessary, telling what he knew of the Domed House, the guard system, the valley itself, the discipline and the probable location of Raemy and Bekart, if prisoners.

The guard was relieved every hour at the temple, and a sharp watch was kept for any movement to attack them. It was dusk when Turk gathered his little group around him.

"Understand this much," he said briefly, "these men are our enemies. They have held American flyers as slaves, they have killed some, tortured others. We must rescue Bob Doone and his sister. We needn't worry about Bekart. He should be punished, but we have enough to do without that. Let's go!"

Dark and cold lay the valley under a high riding moon when the four men reached the icy rim and looked down. The descent to which Young had led them was at the upper end of the long, deep canyon. Far below them, chill and mysterious in the moonlight, lay the towers and rooftops of the monastery and village. Among them all, at the highest level, was the huge dome of the Domed House.

The air was crisp and still. The rattle of a stone sounded loud in the clear, sharp air. Turk rubbed his fingers against the chill and scanned the town below with a practiced, soldier's eye. Young moved up beside him. "So far as I know, nobody's ever tried it from here. It's desperately steep, but working down there on a wall, once, I noticed what seemed to be a path up here. That's our only chance."

"We've got ropes if the wall runs close enough, or if the path doesn't lead all the way around."

"The guards are nearly giants," Young warned. "Big men, and powerfully muscled."

From below came eerie sounds, the strange music drifted to them, then a chanting voice lifted momentarily, high and shrill, yet barely audible where they stood. Uneasily, Shan Bao shifted his feet. Turk's feet felt for the path.

It was actually merely a ledge, only inches wide, where a lower stratum of rock had thrust out and weathering had still to chafe it away.

Turk edged along the rocky lip, his mouth dry. Were they visible from below? He thought not, yet he seemed naked, exposed, helpless. A foot edged out, felt carefully, then his weight shifted, for an instant his hands gripped until his foot was sure, then he moved along.

Hours seemed to pass. Sweat popped out on his face and dried away. The ledge zigged to a lower ledge, which zagged away into darkness under an overhang. They felt their way through the ominous darkness, and found, finally, a place where a spring trickled water into a deep crevice. It seemed a good route, and they followed it.

Darkness closed around them. Turk felt his way, then suddenly, warned by falling water, he stopped. It was well he did, for when he put his foot out it encountered empty space. With a pencil flash, he studied the drop. It fell away far below the reach of the finger of light. He drew back, studying the rocky walls. Finally, he found a way that seemed possible. Then they were on a level again.

Turk had not begun to consider escape. He knew that a wise man never enters any hole or any place of danger without first considering a way out. Yet now there was no chance. What had to be done must be done, and there was no time for details. He moved along and smiled to himself to know that three men moved behind him.

They might have been ghosts wafted by some breeze from beyond the grave for all the sound they made.

The deep crevasse in which they walked ended so suddenly that Turk stopped and Young ran into him. They made no noise, and it was well, for they stood on the edge of a pool, no more than twenty feet across. It was a pool surrounded by shade trees, and now, kneeling on the far side was a girl. She bent down and dipped up water with a wooden bowl, and drank from it. Her face was a delicate tracery of old ivory in the moonlight, and when she put down the bowl she knelt there on the stone slab, gazing up at the moon.

Turk held himself very still. Behind him he could hear the breathing of the other men. Suddenly, and why he did not know, Turk decided he was going to speak to her. Carefully, he moved out from the others and skirted the pond on light stepping feet. When he was no more than a few feet away, he spoke to her gently in Mandarin.

It was a wild chance, but she did not look like a Ngolok woman, nor like a Lolo. At the sound of his voice, she stiffened, and her chin came down, but she did not look at him. She did not turn her head, but looked across the garden. "Who speaks from the willows?" she asked.

He spoke very softly, knowing that now he needed her help, her willing help. "A man who seeks the woman he loves, and her brother, who are prisoners here."

"You are not Chinese?"

"American."

Surprisingly then, she turned her head and spoke in clearest English. "Then speak to me so. I was educated in a mission school and have talked with many Americans."

"You know the prisoner—Bob Doone?"

"Yes, I speak with him often, although it is not allowed." She arose and looked up at Turk. "He is the one you seek?"

"Yes, and the American girl who came today? They did get her, didn't they?"

The girl nodded. "She came in with her hands tied and an American with her. He has been talking with Bo Hau, our master."

"You are a prisoner, too?"

"Yes, they keep me as a hostage to keep the aid of my father, who is in Sining. He sends many caravans here, but he does not like the trade. It is done for my protection."

"You know how we can reach Doone? And his sister?" The others had moved around the pool and stood beside him.

"It cannot be done. They are guarded with great care. Bo Hau has wanted something from the American. The man who came today with the woman, I heard him say he could show them how to get it. That he would help."

"By torturing her in front of her brother!" Young said. He swore bitterly. "To think the guy was once on our side! That we ate at the same mess!"

Turk shook his head. "We cannot accept your decision that it cannot be done. It must be done, and tonight, we'll do it."

She nodded as one who understands when a decision is irrevocable. "Then I will take you there," she said, "but what of the guards?"

Turk put his hand on her shoulder. "You take us," he said gently, "we'll cross our guards when we get to them!"

Without further hesitation she turned and led them across the garden. Had they traveled by any other route than down the water course there would have been walls to climb, but here the gardens of the Domed House ran right against the mountain itself.

Her way took them to a door set in a high wall. She opened it and went in, leading them across a paved court where they moved silently. At the far wall she hesitated. "I will speak to the guard," she said, "and then—"

Silently, Shan Bao glided to the fore. "And then I shall act!" he said, low-voiced.

She opened the door and passed within, but when she had taken five steps she paused and turned slightly, then she spoke softly in some strange tongue. The guard stepped toward her, answering with a question. Swiftly, Shan Bao moved in, but some scarcely audible sound must have come to the guard. He wheeled, grasping his huge sword. Yet big as he was and fast as he was, he had no chance. The Manchu was too close, and his deadly knife darted like a serpent's tongue and the big man fell forward. Shan Bao used the knife once more, and then they moved on.

Young breathed into Madden's ear, "You have that guy around all the time?"

Turk nodded. He started to speak, then stopped, for now they were entering a long, dank passageway that trended down in a long steep ramp. When they had gone a hundred yards they began to pass barred doors.

"Slaves," the girl whispered, "slaves, and most of them Chinese or Lolos. There is another guard ahead, then the men prisoners. The girl is kept above stairs."

Hardly had she finished speaking when a huge man loomed around the corner ahead of them. His eyes widened and his mouth opened for a bellow that would have rocked the monastery, but Turk was moving. Lunging like a fullback, he plowed into the big guard before the man could lift his sword, and, knocked from his hands, it hit the floor with a loud clang.

The huge man grabbed at Madden, but Turk slipped inside of those mighty hands and smashed a right to the guard's heart with every ounce of his two hundred pounds of whipcord and steel muscle behind it. The big man staggered and went back on his hands and knees.

"The prisoners!" Turk snapped crisply at Sparrow Ryan. "Don't bother about me! Go get Doone!"

The guard rushed, and Turk came to his feet, weaved inside the huge hands, and slashed the Ngolok's face with a lancing left hand, and then he began throwing punches with every ounce of power he had. Smashing the guard back with a wicked overhand right, he hooked a left and right to the body. Wildly, the guard swung, but Madden was inside and fighting for his life. He stabbed a right to the body, then lifted his hand and hacked the edge of it across the guard's Adam's apple!

Gagging horribly, the guard fell to his knees and Madden smashed him to the floor. Then he rolled the big man over and, ripping off the rawhide string he used for a belt, lashed the man's hands behind him. Then he bound his feet together and hurriedly gagged him with a corner of the padded cloth ripped from the man's clothing.

Bob Doone—Turk knew him at once from his resemblance to Raemy—lunged from a cell. A half dozen other followed from other cells. The Chinese girl was hastily motioning them on, so wiping the sweat from his face, Turk started after her. The others fell in behind.

Now she led them up a steep, winding stair into a wide stone hall. Then up another stair. Suddenly, Turk paused. "Ryan," he said, "you'd better take Doone and get out. Get that steel box!"

"And leave you? Don't be crazy!"

"You've got a job to do!" Turk told him. "Besides, I'll have Shan. From now on, it's up to me. Don't tell Bob I'm after Raemy."

Ryan hesitated, then shrugged. With Young he turned back. Turk walked on down the empty passage behind the slim young Chinese girl. Suddenly, she gestured at him and stepped into a doorway at one side of the passage. Turk and Shan Bao followed, and no sooner were they concealed than four of the big guards appeared, and marching between them were Raemy and Bekart!

Watching, they saw the group turn into a wide doorway and vanish into a room. Turk hesitated a moment, his mind working swiftly. From all appearances the prisoners were being taken to a questioning. This would be the one big chance: when they were not locked in cells!

The long passage was dank and gloomy. Certainly, if modern tendencies were alive among the Ngoloks, they had done little to improve their living conditions. A chill pervaded the great Domed House, the damp, empty chill of a building long cold.

This was no secret and marvelous lost civilization, it was the den of a barbaric people, constructed long ago, and almost untouched since. The flagstone floor was uneven and dirt gathered in the cracks. Here and there dampness had left stains on the walls and ceiling.

"You'd better go back to the garden," Turk whispered to the girl. "We'll come that way and take you with us!"

He stepped out of his hiding place boldly and walked across to the huge plank door. Without a glance over his shoulder he lifted the latch and stepped within. He heard the light slap of Shan Bao's footsteps behind him and heard the door close softly. He did not turn his head, for his eyes were riveted upon the great hall in which he stood.

They were under the vast dome, and suspended from it was a huge bronze bell!

Towering high under the great dome, the bell was enormous, and across the bottom, which was a mere eight feet from the stone floor, it was fully as wide as it was tall! Directly beneath it was a chair, bolted to the floor. Four of the huge Ngolok tribesmen stripped to the waist stood around the bell, each with a huge mallet. The bell had no clapper, but was to be sounded by blows from the Ngoloks.

Several steps below the bell were Raemy Doone and Travis Bekart. Two guards stood beside them, and facing them was a woman, tall, and thin to emaciation, her face a haglike mask of wickedness and cunning. Behind her was a big man who could be none other than Bo Hau.

The entry of Turk and Shan Bao had been unnoticed as there was a screen before the door to prevent the entry of evil spirits, which according to the Ngolok belief must travel in a straight line and so cannot get around a screen.

Madden took in the scene at a glance. He needed no explanation for the chair beneath the bell. There was no form of torture so quickly calculated to ruin a man's self-possession, none that would drive him into insanity and death so quickly as the awful roar of sound and the vibration. Beneath that bell the vibration would be terrific and centered entirely on that chair.

The guard nearest Raemy took her by the arm and started her for the chair, and then Turk stepped around from behind the screen. His heart jumping, he started toward them. He had taken three steps before Bo Hau looked up, and their eyes met.

"Release her!" Turk commanded.

The old queen's eyes lit with an insane humor. "Kill him!" she said, her tone flat and cold.

The guard near Bekart wheeled, lifting his rifle. Turk's hand shot out and grasped the rifle barrel underneath, then his left hand dropped to the stock just back of the breech. He jerked back with his left hand and shoved up hard with his right and ripped the rifle from the astonished guard's hands. The man sprawled on the floor, and Turk stepped back, his rifle on the queen.

One flickering instant, no more. "Release her," he repeated.

The guard holding Raemy took his hands away from her. Bo Hau was staring at Turk, his eyes alive with fanatic hatred.

"Raemy," Turk said, his eyes shifting from Bo Hau to the queen, "walk back to the door!"

"Aren't you taking me?" Bekart demanded.

"Why should we?" Madden replied harshly. "So you can stand trial for murdering your fellow soldiers?"

"Take me with you!" Bekart pleaded. "Don't leave me here! These people are fiends!"

"You escaped us and went to them," Turk's voice was level.

"But, man! You can't—"

"All right!" Turk relented. "Get along, but one wrong move and I'll shoot you myself!"

Bekart jerked free and ran after Raemy. Slowly, Turk began to back up. In all this time, scarcely more than two minutes at most, Bo Hau had said nothing.

Ngoloks gathered around the bell had moved forward slowly, their eyes on Madden. The man on the floor got slowly to his feet. Turk watched them as he moved back, knowing that Shan Bao covered him, yet wary.

The old woman was scarcely sane. A withered hag, eaten by hatred, her mind twisted by power, and probably in a measure dominated by Bo Hau.

The big Ngolok was grinning now. "You go?" he spoke suddenly, pleasantly. His voice was high-pitched. "You leave so soon? We should so like to have you stay for dinner. Is it not the custom among your people to invite guests to stay for dinner?"

Turk did not reply, and suddenly Bo Hau's face was ugly with anger. "Kill him!" he snapped.

The other guard's rifle swung up, and even as it lifted, Turk swung the rifle he held and fired from the hip. The guard's rifle clattered on the floor, he clutched wildly at his stomach, and pitched over on the stone floor.

"Thank you!" Bo Hau said brightly. "Now my people will come . . . thousands of them!"

Somewhere a gong clanged with huge, hammering blows, and the great Domed House was filled with a clamor of voices mingling with the roar of the gong and running feet!

"Run!" Turk roared at Shan Bao. "Back the way we came!"

Darting down the long hall, they rounded the turn to see a guard looming in the way. Turk's rifle bellowed and the guard went down screaming. From behind them there was a shout, then a shot. The bullet ricocheted from the wall. When they reached the garden, still bright and glorious in the glow of the young moon, Turk stopped. "Take them, Shan!" he said. "Make it quick!"

For an instant, the Manchu hesitated, and Raemy's lips started to form a protest, then they were moving.

Madden walked back and picked up a rifle by the wall where the guard was bound, and with it his ammunition belt. Then he retreated to the rocks on the far side of the pool. Kneeling behind the rocks, he waited.

His mouth was dry and his heart was pounding, but he tried to calm himself. The gate burst open suddenly, and men poured through it. Resting the rifle stock against his cheek, Turk began to squeeze off his shots. Once—twice—three times!

Each time a man fell, and the attack broke and split to either side among the shrubbery. Another man showed in the doorway, and Turk fired again. The man crumpled and fell. He shifted his position and studied the shrubbery. A slight movement warned him, but he waited. Suddenly a man lunged from the nearest bush, a huge knife in his hand. With a scream, he hurled himself at Turk's breastwork!

The rifle barked again, and knocked back by the force of the heavy bullet, the Ngolok toppled into the pool. In the breathing space, Turk reloaded the rifle. Then, carefully, he eased back into the shadows.

Shan would be leading them up the steep climb again by now. He moved back, felt a rock wall, and then a low voice, Ryan's, came to him. "Turk?"

"Yeah!"

"That Chinese gal showed us a new way out. Old steps in the cliff, used years ago. I waited to guide you. They comin' after us yet?"

"In a couple of minutes. I got a few of them, scared 'em a little. Let's go!"

Sparrow Ryan led the way, and they hurried up the steep steps as behind them there was a flurry of movement. Far up the stair Turk heard a stone rattle.

Suddenly, torches were burning behind them, and they could hear shouts and yells as the searching party scrambled through the dark crevasse. Ryan rushed on ahead. Turk turned at a small landing and glanced back. He could see the bobbing torches. Coolly and with care he began to fire.

A torch toppled and a scream lifted. Again and again he fired until the rifle was empty, and then he coolly reloaded and emptied it once more. Then he turned away.

A shadow moved, then the huge, greasy body of one of the mallet holders who had stood by the bell loomed from the shadows. How he got there, Turk could only guess. By some secret stair, no doubt, that opened upon this same landing.

The man was a veritable giant, stripped to the waist with his massive muscles gleaming in the light of the moon. Turk's tongue touched his lips, and he circled warily as the man crouched and came toward him. Accustomed too long to fighting with his hands, he forgot his pistol, forgot everything but the huge man who moved toward him, catlike on his huge sandal-clad feet.

Suddenly, the Ngolok lunged. Turk's left fist *splatted* against his lips, and Madden felt the give of the big man's teeth, but then the fellow had his hands on him, and they slipped around his body, wrapping him in a pythonlike grip!

Turk's head jerked forward and smashed into the Ngolok's face, but then the big man jerked his head aside and began to crush with powerful arms. Turk's left hand was bound to his side by the encircling arms but with his right he hooked short and hard to the ear, then struck down on the kidney with the edge of his hand. The Ngolok grunted, but heaved harder with his powerful arms. Agonizing pain shot through Turk, and he struggled wildly to get loose, then his right lifted and he dug his thumb into the big man's mouth, keeping it between his cheek and the side of his teeth. Digging all four fingers into the flesh behind the giant's ear and jawbone, he jerked back with all his strength!

The Ngolok screamed hoarsely as his cheek ripped under the tearing thumb, and his grip relaxed. As it did, Turk lifted his knee and stomped down on the huge sandal-clad foot with all his strength. With a roar of pain, the big man let go, and Turk sprang back, staggered, and then setting himself, swung a right hand that had the works on it. The punch caught the huge man off balance and he toppled back, hit the crumbling stone parapet, and went over in a shower of falling stones, his screams echoing upward through the vast chimney where they had climbed.

His back stiff with pain, Turk started on up the stair, his lungs gasping for air, his brain wild with fear of what lay behind. Somehow he reached the top and found Ryan crouching there, awaiting him.

The air on the high plateau was crisp and cold, and he gasped great draughts into his tortured lungs. Then he turned and they stumbled away into the darkness together.

Several minutes more and they came up with the rest of the party. Young walked a step behind Bekart, his eyes never wavering from the former pursuit pilot's back. Raemy's face was drawn and pale. Turk caught up with her, and she noted his torn shirt and a dark stain of blood on his cheek where the Ngolok's clawing hand had torn the flesh like a claw. "You're hurt!"

"No, and we've got to keep going," he said. "Can you make it?"

"I think so."

Turk's eyes strayed to the Chinese girl. She was walking along, patiently, quietly. He knew the look. He had seen it in the faces of Chinese infantrymen long ago. They would walk until they dropped.

Scotty met them in the hills with a half dozen armed men. He grinned at Turk, then looked quickly at Doone. "You all right?"

Bob Doone was walking beside his sister. He looked up and grinned. He was very thin, but his eyes were very bright. "Sure!" he said. "Who could be better?"

A silent group met in the big room where the Goose waited, resting easily on the dark water. Young, Scotty, Doone, Ryan, and Kalinov gathered around Turk. He was brief and to the point.

"We've got to move out—now! They'll be down here, and we haven't weapons enough to fight them off. Scotty, I'd say you and Kalinov should move out right away, keep to the low country and get as much distance between you and this bunch as you can. It'll be rough going, but you'll have to do it.

"Travel light. We haven't much in the way of supplies, but

we'll rustle some more and bring them to you, supply you by
air.

"Don't fight unless you have to, but keep your riflemen to
the rear."

Madden watched them go, scowling thoughtfully. He was
worried by Bo Hau's lack of opposition to the escape from the
Domed House. The man had the look of a plotter, a conniver
as well as a man of action. Turk doubted that they would get
away so easily.

The Grumman had brought more supplies than needed, and
a few things were carried by the walking party, which made
the plane somewhat lighter. There remained Young, Doone,
Ryan, Shan, Bekart, and the two girls. It was still a heavy load.
Madden had his own plans, intending to fly the fighter. From
what he originally learned, there was still another fighter and
two transports somewhere around the valley.

The transports, even if armed, did not worry him. The
fighter was another thing.

Bob Doone had avoided Bekart, and he avoided him now as
he walked over to where Turk Madden, his thumbs tucked
behind his belt, was staring bleakly at the grim hills. The gray
clouds had lowered themselves over the peaks now, and the
massive grandeur of Amne Machin was shut out.

"Ryan tells me you came for my cargo, too?" Bob suggested.

Turk nodded. "And the sooner we get it and get moving, the
better."

"All right. When you're ready, I'll take you to it. I hid it
myself."

"Sparrow, you come with us. Shan, get the ship warmed up.
Young, if you will, warm up the fighter for me. I'm flying it."
He glanced at the Manchu. "And keep an eye on Bekart. He's
got something on his mind!"

Turk checked his Colt, and then the three turned and walked
from the ancient temple. The wind outside was raw and chill.
Bob Doone led off and they started up the street, over the
tumbled walls and broken stones. When they were halfway up
the hill they stopped and looked back. White caps dotted the
lake's black water, and the hills were a sullen gray and black,
streaked here and there in cracks and crevices with the white
of snow.

On the far side of a plateau a path led downward. "Found it

by accident," Doone said. "Came down here, couldn't carry the box very far. Before we crashed I'd seen those natives coming, and they didn't look enticing."

The path dipped into a thick growth of pine, then out and into a small open glade at the end of a canyon. Here, set away by itself, was a temple.

A wide stone-flagged terrace lay before it. They walked across, footsteps echoing hollowly, then up three high steps and through the narrow door.

Inside, the light was vague, but they could see a bare and empty room except for one place at a far corner where some animal had gathered sticks and grass for a nest. A huge figure of what was intended for Buddha loomed at the end. They walked toward it, and Doone gestured. "See? The Buddha is newer than the rest. Probably some other god was there and they put the Buddha in its place. Didn't work very well from what I heard in the valley, for the people deserted the temple and, later, the town."

He circled the pedestal and the huge stone figure. "Careful! It's balanced very badly there. I think someone started to move it, planning to return the original, and then stopped."

It was not of one solid stone, rather of blocks cunningly fitted together.

Behind the pedestal, Doone got down on his knees and dug at a flat block fitted into the floor. Using a knife, he succeeded in getting his fingers under the edge. He heaved on the slab, and his shoulder touched the pedestal. The figure above teetered dangerously. "Look out!" Ryan warned. "If that thing fell off of there it would kill us all!"

Turk stooped and got one edge of the slab and they lifted it out. In the recess below was the black steel box. Carefully, they lifted it out.

Turk and Ryan each took a handle, and they straightened. Turk went suddenly cold inside. His right hand gripped the handle on the steel box, his Colt was in its shoulder holster in his left armpit. And Travis Bekart was standing before them, in his hands a submachine gun. He was smiling, his coldly handsome face was even colder now, and his eyes were like ice. "So," he said, "here's the payoff! Didn't think I'd let you get away with this, did you, Madden? You messed up my plans for me. I'd an idea of marrying Raemy and living on the fat of the land, then getting rid of her and inheriting it all myself. I got Doone out of the way, and then you had to nose in.

"But I'd no intention of going back as a prisoner. Oh, no! I intend to go back, all right! I'll go back alone, and very sad that you were lost, but I'll take the black box with me, and they will be very pleased. I may even get a decoration for it. And there will be other women with money."

"What about Young?" Doone said. "He knows!"

"Young is dead," Bekart replied, with triumph. "I've killed him. I pushed Raemy into the lake when no one was looking, then when the Manchu went in after her, I took this gun and came away. Unfortunately Young never knew what hit him. And now you . . . you'll all know, and I'll have made a clean sweep. I'll just leave the girls. Those Ngoloks will take care of them. It will serve Raemy right for not marrying me when she had the chance."

"You talk a lot," Turk said. If only he didn't have that damned box! He could make a try for his gun and—

Bob Doone shifted his feet. "You can't get away with it," he said. He shifted his right foot a little, lost his balance, and hurled his weight against the pedestal of the huge Buddha!

As his weight hit the pedestal there was a grinding crash from the stone rollers beneath the figure and the great mass of stone toppled forward!

Travis Bekart threw up his arms with a scream of fear as he saw the huge stone figure looming over him. For one blinding instant the man's face was a tortured white mask, and then with a mighty crash the stone image hit the man's widespread arms and screaming face, burying him under an avalanche of ancient granite.

The sound died, dust lifted, and Turk staggered forward, pulling on his handle of the box. "Let's go!" he said.

They found Young down on his face beside the fighter, his head smashed with the heavy slugs.

"Go ahead," Turk told them. "Get this into the amphibian and take off. Get moving."

Tenderly, he carried the man's body to a place beside the other grave. He scraped out a hollow and rolled the body into it, then covered it with brush and stones. There was no time to make a cross.

He turned and hurried back to the fighter. As he did so, he caught a movement on the lake front below, and saw a column of men circling the lake toward the temple!

Yet even as he looked, he saw the amphibian taxi out on the water. Scrambling into the fighter, he revved the motors. Young had evidently had them warmed fairly well before he was killed. Staring at the lake front, he saw the monks begin to deploy along the waterfront, scattering out in a crude skirmishing line.

Twin motors roaring, he started the ship down the plateau. It bumped, then rolled faster and faster. Swiftly, he shot over the packed snow, then hauled back on the stick and lifted the tiny ship. He was airborne. He climbed steadily, then swung around in a steep bank and raced back for the lake front.

He could see the monks lifting their rifles now, and although he could hear no sound, he knew they were firing. Then he swept down upon them and tripped the triggers on his guns. The leading edge of the wing burst into fire, and he saw the scattered line break and lunge for cover. One man leaped off into the icy water, and then Turk came back on the stick and shot away above the lake, lifting higher and higher, reaching for altitude to put him above the amphibian. The plane below him was heading off across the bleak gray hills, and a thousand feet higher he turned after the fleet Grumman.

He turned once, to glance back toward the valley, and his eye caught a flash of movement. He glanced up, and fear struck him like a blow! Another fighter was dropping out of the gray clouds, guns flaming, and coming down in a wild, screaming dive!

Turk whipped the fighter around and dove for the lake, then shot up, just clearing the black edge of the surrounding ridge by a matter of feet. The enemy fighter was on his tail and coming fast. He swung the ship again, darting this way and that in a mad rush to escape. A bullet hole appeared in the instrument panel ahead of him, and something spattered on his face.

He hauled back on the stick and climbed almost straight up toward the gray clouds, then went over backward in a loop,

trying to reverse positions, but as he swept by the other ship
he saw a fleeting glimpse of a taut yellowish face! *Bo Hau!*

A burst of tracer flamed past him and he whipped the ship
around, fighting for his life. The big Ngolok knew his ship and
knew every trick of flying. Another burst, and Turk felt a sharp
blow on his leg. There was no chance to glance down, but
feeling numb and sick, he whipped the ship around again and
dove like a streak for the dark, stone-filled streets below!

As he eased out of a screaming dive he shot the ship for the
looming black tower and banked around as if rounding a pylon
on a racing course, Bo Hau whipped around it, too, but with a
sudden loop, at its bottom no more than fifty feet above the
black stone roofs, Turk got Bo Hau's fighter in his sights,
and he let go a burst that riddled the engine cowling and
cockpit. The fighter dipped suddenly and went crashing into
the street, one wing ripping off as it hit the edge of a stone
roof.

There was a tremendous burst of flame, and an explosion
that rocked Turk's fighter, and then he was speeding away,
heading after the amphibian.

His motors began to stutter, then spit, and he leveled off and
headed for the ground. Ahead was a long level stretch, rocky
and scattered here and there with dark, dry-looking brush. As
he came in, he cut his speed, eased back a bit on the stick, felt
her wheels touch, then again, and then the ship hit a bush and
the tail flopped up and over.

Something smashed him on the head, and he conked out.

After a long time, he opened his eyes. He was hanging in his
safety belt, one shoulder against the edge of the seat. Holding on
with one hand, he loosened the safety belt and topped to the
ground below. He sat there for a long time, his head buzzing.
Then he got to his feet, gathered up the few things that
belonged to him, and started on weaving feet down the trail
the marching party had taken.

Sometime during the night he fell down by a bush and slept,
and then almost at dawn the cold awakened him. Turk staggered to his feet, staring around him. His head throbbed and
he was tired, but his mind was clear. Of all that had happened
since he began walking he had no idea, nor where he was. He
saw the tracks of a considerable party and started on, putting
each foot down with care.

*   *   *

At noon, somewhere between delirium and sanity, he heard a hum in the sky and looked up, shielding his eyes. Then it stopped and he walked on. He was walking like that when they found him, Sparrow Ryan and Raemy.

He was walking solemnly along the dim trail, his eyes fixed ahead of him, blood all over his head and caked in his hair and on his cheek, limping with one leg, but walking on.

Raemy saw him first, and she started to run. "Oh, Turk! Turk! I thought you were *dead!*"

Her arms went around him and he felt her soft lips on his and through the fog of pain his memory came back and he looked over her red-gold hair at Ryan, who was grinning with relief.

"Go away!" he said. "Can't you see she wants to be alone?"

AUTHOR'S NOTE
The Goose Flies South

More on mercenaries:

For thousands of years warfare offered a young man his best chance of advancement. Because of the rigid caste system that existed in Europe, the chances for an ambitious man were slight unless he went to war, where courage and a strong arm might win him riches, a knighthood, or a place among the great captains of his time.

In Ireland in the time of Queen Elizabeth, there was no future for a young Irishman of family, so many sailed away to Europe to take service in one army or another. Because they flew away to far lands they were called "wild geese." Alexander O'Reilly, who commanded the Spanish army for a time, was one such. General McMahon, who served with Napoleon, was another. There were Irish soldiers in every army in Europe, as well as in Latin America.

Often such soldiers moved from war to war as long as they survived, renewing old acquaintances as they moved. Yet, often enough it was harder to collect the money promised than it was to win the war, if such wars are ever won.

It was a hard world, yet few such men knew any other, and nobody mourns for a mercenary.

Nor does a mercenary expect it.

THE GOOSE FLIES SOUTH

Steadily the motors were droning away, in the thin upper air. "If I was a betting man," Panola said grimly, "I'd give ten to one we never get out of this alive!"

"You asked for it!" Captain Runnels replied dryly. "This is strictly volunteer stuff. You could have ducked it."

"Sure," Panola shrugged. "But who wants to duck a job like this? I asked for it, but I'm not dumb!"

Turk Madden eased forward on the stick and felt the Goose let her nose down. In the heavy, cottony mass of cloud you could see less than nothing. Letting her down was taking a real chance, but they were almost at their destination, and they would soon be ready to land.

There were a lot of jagged peaks here, many of them running upwards of two thousand feet. He was already below that level and saw no sign of an opening to the world below.

The Goose dipped out of the clouds suddenly, and with a rush. A huge, craggy, and black mountainside towered above them. Turk whipped the Grumman over in a steep bank and swung away from the cliff, missing it by inches. He glanced at Winkler as the ship flattened out. The Major's face was a sickly yellow.

"Close, that!" he said grimly.

"It was," Turk grinned. "You don't see 'em much closer."

He glanced over his shoulder. Runnels and Panola looked scared, but Shan Bao, his mechanic and righthand man, a tall Manchu, seemed undisturbed. Death itself meant little to the Manchu.

"How much farther?" Runnels asked, leaning forward.

"Not far. We just sighted Mount Stokes, so it'll be just a few minutes."

"Let's hope the place is empty," Panola said. "We'd be in a spot if some ship was lying there."

"It's pretty safe," Turk said. "Nothing down here to speak of, and even less back inland. All this section of the Argentine and Chile is wild and lonely. South, it gets even worse."

It was a cold, bleak, and barren country, sullen and dreary under the heavy gray overcast. Great craggy peaks lifted into the low clouds, and below there were occasional inlets, most of them edged with angry foam. Some of the mountains were covered with trees, and in places the forest came down to the water's edge. In other places there were only bleak plains, wind blown and rain whipped.

Then suddenly he saw the mountain, a huge, black, domelike peak that shouldered into the clouds.

"That's the Dome of St. Paul," he said, looking over at Winkler. "San Esteban Gulf is right close by."

He swung the plane inland, skirting the long sandy beach on which a furious surf was breaking, sighted San Quentin Bay with its thickly wooded shores, and then swung across toward the mouth of the San Tadeo River.

The land about the river mouth was low and marshy and covered with stumps of dead trees, some of them truly gigantic in size. Inside the mouth of the river it widened to considerable breadth, and something like seven miles up it divided into two rivers. Turk swung the ship up the course of the Black River, flying low. The stream was choked with the trunks of dead trees, and huge roots that thrust themselves out of the water like the legs of gigantic spiders.

A few miles farther, and then he swung inland above a barely discernible brook, and then eased forward on the stick and let the amphibian come down on the smooth surface of the small lake. He taxied across toward a cove lined with heavy timber, and then let the ship swing around as he dropped the anchor in comparative shelter.

"Wow!" Panola shook his head and grinned at Turk as the latter peeled off his flying helmet. "How you ever remembered this place is beyond me! How long since you were here?"

"Twelve years," Madden replied. "I was a kid then, just going to sea. Incidentally, from here on we'd better go armed.

I'm just giving you a tip, although of course, that's up to Major Winkler."

"We'll go armed," Winkler said. "And all of you know, we can't take any chances on being found. We've got to get this plane under cover and stay there ourselves as much as possible. If we were caught here, there's not a chance we'd get out of this alive."

Turk watched Shan Bao getting out the rubber boat and then turned his gaze toward the mainland. The amphibian lay in a small cove, excellently sheltered on all sides. The entrance to the cove from the small lake was an S-shaped waterway, ending in a pool. The pool was surrounded on all sides by a heavy growth of timber. It was a mixture of fir, pine, and occasional beech trees. The beach was sandy and littered with washed up roots and trunks of old trees.

There was no sign of life of any kind. And that was as it should be. Not over two dozen men on earth knew that here, off the coast of Patagonia, was to be another experiment with an atomic bomb. An experiment kept secret from the world, and of which no American from the North, no Englishman, and no Russian was to know. It was an experiment being made by a few desperate and skillful German scientists and military men, working with power-mad militarists of the Argentine.

Turk Madden, soldier of fortune, adventurer, and late officer in the Military Intelligence, was flying his own plane, a special-built Grumman Goose with a number of improvements and a greater armament and flying range than the ordinary Goose. The trip was in command of Major Winkler, and with them were Captain Runnels and Lieutenant Panola, a recently discharged officer.

Runnels and Winkler were both skilled atomic specialists. Panola was the record man whose task it would be to compile and keep the records of the trip and of the secret experiments, if they were able to observe them. Shan Bao, the Manchu, was Madden's own Man Friday, a hard-bitten North China fighter whom Turk had met in Siberia.

Turk, Winkler, and Runnels went ashore first.

"We've got to set up a shelter," Winkler suggested. "And the sooner the better, as it may rain. What would you suggest, Madden? You've had more of this sort of experience than I."

"Back in the woods," he said instantly. "Find four living

trees for the corner posts. Clear out under them and build walls of some of these dead logs we see around. If we cut trees, the white blaze of the cut will be visible from the air. You can spot 'em for miles in the right light. But there's enough brush here, and we shouldn't have to cut anything except under the four trees."

The place he selected was four huge trees with wide spreading branches near a huge, rocky outcropping. There was nothing but brush between the trees, and it was a matter of minutes for the five men to clear it away. Then they began hauling up logs from the beach. Several of them were large enough to split into four timbers. By nightfall they had the walls erected and a peaked roof of interwoven bows with fir limbs covering it. All was safely under the spreading branches of the trees.

Turk paced the beach restlessly, and his eyes studied the low hanging clouds. The whole thing had been too easy, and he was worried. The ship that had brought them south had heaved to on a leaden sea, and the amphibian had been put into the water. Then, with their equipment and supplies aboard, they had taken off. The whole process, planned and carefully rehearsed, had taken them no more than minutes.

On the flight to the mainland they had seen no one, no ship, no boat, nothing remotely human. Yet even on this lonely shore, it seemed too easy.

It was miles to the nearest port. The country inland was wild and broken, no country for a man to live in. Yet here and there were Patagonian savages, he knew. And there might be others. Knowing the cold-blooded ruthless tactics of his enemy, and their thoroughness, he could not but doubt.

When the logs had been moved from the beach, he carefully picked up any chips and covered the places where they had lain with as much skill as possible.

A spring flowed from the rock outcropping near the house they had built. They could reach it without going into the open. They had food enough, although he knew there had once been a few deer in the vicinity. Otherwise, there would be nothing except occasional sea birds, and perhaps a hair seal or two.

Runnels, a heavyset, brown-faced man who had been working with atomic scientists for ten years, walked toward him.

"Beastly lonely place, isn't it? Reminds me of the Arctic. I hunted in Dawson once."

Madden nodded. "Seems too good to be true," he said thoughtfully, "I smell trouble!"

"You're pessimistic!" Runnels said. His face grew serious. "Well, if it comes we can't do a thing but take it. We're on our own. They told us if we got caught, we couldn't expect any help from home."

"What's the dope on this experiment?" Turk asked. "I don't know much about it."

"They've got two old German warships. Ships that got away before the rest were surrendered. They are in bad shape, but good enough for the experiment. They are going to try sinking them with an atomic bomb about two hundred miles off shore. Then, they are going to try an experiment inland, back in the waste of the plains.

"Our job is not to interfere, only to get information on the results so we can try a comparison with our own."

Turk Madden nodded. He had his own orders. He had been told to obey orders from Winkler up to a point, beyond that his own judgment counted most as he was the most experienced at this sort of thing. Also, if it were possible, he was to try to destroy whatever equipment or bombs they had. But that was his own job and was to be done with utmost skill, and entirely without giving away his presence or that of his party.

A difficult, almost impossible mission, but one that could be done. After all, he had blown bridges right under the noses of the Japanese. This could scarcely be more difficult.

He walked toward the ridge and, keeping under the trees, climbed slowly toward the top. Now was the time to get acquainted with the country. There was one infallible rule for warfare or struggle of any kind—know your terrain—and he intended to know this.

There were no paths, but he found a way toward the top along a broken ledge, a route that he noticed was not visible from below, if the traveler would but move with reasonable care to avoid being seen. There were broken slabs of rock, and much undergrowth.

He was halfway up before the path became difficult, and then he used his hands to pull himself from handhold to handhold. Yet, before he had reached the top, he slipped suddenly and began to slide downward with rapidly increasing momentum.

Below him was a cliff which he had skirted. Wildly, his hand shot out to stay his fall. It closed upon a bush, and—held.

Slowly, carefully, fearful at each instant that the bush would come loose at the roots, he pulled himself up until he had a foothold. Then a spot of blackness arrested his eye. It was a hole.

Moving carefully, to get a better view, he found it was a small hole in the rock, a spot scarcely large enough to admit a man's body. Taking out his flashlight, he thrust his arm inside, and gasped with surprise.

Instead of a small hole, it was a large cavern, a room of rock bigger than the shelter below, and with a black hole leading off into dimness beyond the reach of his light.

Thoughtfully, he withdrew his arm. Turning his head, he looked below. He could see the pool where the plane was, and he could see the lake. But he was not visible from the shelter. Nor, if he remained still, could he be seen from below.

He pulled himself higher and began once more to climb. Why, he did not know, but suddenly he decided he would say nothing of the cave. Later, perhaps. But not now.

When Madden reached the crest of the hill he did not stand up. He had pulled himself over the rim and was lying face down. Carefully, he inched along the ground until he was behind a large bush. He rose to his knees and carefully brushed off his clothes. Then he looked.

He was gazing over a wide, inland valley. About two miles away was another chain of hills still higher. The valley itself led away inland, a wide sweep with a small stream flowing through it. A stream that was obviously a tributary leading to the Rio Negro.

North along the coast were great, massive headlands, brutal shoulders of rock of a gloomy grandeur but rarely seen elsewhere. The hills where there was soil were covered with evergreens and with antarctic beeches in thick growth.

Under those trees moss grew heavy, so thick and heavy that one could sink knee deep into it, and there was thick undergrowth also. Yet, a knowing man could move swiftly even in that incredible tangle.

Turk started down the ridge upon which he had lain, sure now that nobody was in sight. Indeed, there was scarcely a chance that a man had been in this area in months, if not in years. He walked swiftly, headed for a promontory not far away where he might have a better view up the coast.

He had dropped from a rocky ledge and turned around a huge boulder when he saw something that brought him up short. For an instant, his eyes swept the area before him, a small, flat plain leading to the foot of the bluff toward which he had been going. There was nothing. Nothing now. Yet there upon the turf of the plain were the clear, unmistakable tracks of wheels!

Turk walked swiftly to the tracks, yet careful to step on stones, of which there were plenty, and thus leave no track himself. Then he stopped, staring at the tracks.

A plane. A fighter craft by the distance between the tires, and the weight as indicated by the impression left on the turf. If not a fighter, then a small plane, heavily loaded. More likely, a fighter. The landing here would not be bad.

Yet why here?

Carefully, and with infinite skill, he began to skirt the plain, examining every nook, every corner. Finally, he found a dead fire. He touched his hand to the ashes. There was, he thought, a bare suggestion of warmth.

He looked around at the camp site. Someone had stopped here, picked up wood, and built the fire. They had warmed a lunch, eaten, and then flown away.

Four small logs had been placed side by side, and the fire built upon them, thus the fire was kept off the damp ground. One of the men, and there had been two, had known something. He was a woodsman. At least, he was not unfamiliar with the wilds. That meant even more care must be exercised.

He shifted his carbine to his left hand and studied the scene thoughtfully. Was the visit here an accident? Had there been a mere forced landing? Or was it by intention?

Squatting on his haunches, he studied the ends of the sticks the fire had left unburned. Several of them were fresh, white and newly cut. But several were older, older and yet as he dug into the bark with his thumbnail, he saw they were still green.

It could mean but one thing. Someone had been here more than once. Someone had built a fire here before. Turning, he walked back to the tracks, and working carefully, he moved across the plain. He found two more sets of tracks.

So that was it. A patrol plane. A plane that flew along this bit of coast, stopped here occasionally while the pilot and his companions cooked and ate a warm meal, probably loafed awhile, and then took off again.

It meant more than that. It meant the Americans had slipped in but a short time after the patrol plane had left. That the fact they were alive at all was due to the fact that Turk Madden had touched the coast south of the San Tadeo River. Had he come right in over the coast they would have met the fighter plane! Or have missed it by the narrowest of margins!

Turk turned quickly, but even as he turned, something whipped by his face and hit the tree behind him with a *thud*!

Madden hit the ground all in one piece and rolled into the brush. Instantly, he was on his hands and knees and crawling. He made a dozen yards to the right before he stopped behind the trunk of a huge beech and stared out across the open.

Almost at once there were four more quick shots. Four shots openly spaced and timed, and Turk heard one of them clip through the trees on his left, and the second flipped by him so close that he dropped flat and hugged the ground, his face white and his spine chilled by the close escape.

The other two shots clipped through the woods some distance off.

"Smart guy, eh?" Turk snarled. "Two shots evenly spaced on each side of where I hit the brush! You're not so dumb!"

Straightening up, he stood behind the tree and studied the situation. It was late, and it was cloudy. By the time he had skirted the plain it would be pitch dark, and he could find no tracks, while he was certain to make some noise and the chances of his being shot, if his assailant waited, would be great.

Walking back over the country between the campfire and the hidden base, he scowled over the problem. Who could be in the vicinity? Had one of the men with the plane remained behind? But if so, why? That didn't make sense, for even if the enemy were expecting something of the kind, they would never expect it right here. Quite obviously, the entire coast was patrolled, probably as much against their own people, if any, as against foreigners.

If someone had remained behind in that vast and lonely country it could mean but one thing: They had been betrayed.

And if it wasn't a stranger, it could be only one of the men of his own party! Yet, if so, why shoot? They were anxious to keep their presence concealed. Could there be a traitor in his own group?

When he stepped through the door into the shelter under the trees, they were all there. Shan Bao was stewing something in a kettle over the fire. He glanced up, but said nothing.

Runnels grinned at him. "Well, we beat you back, but not by very long!"

Turk looked at him for a moment. "You were out, too?"

"Yeah, all of us. We decided it was as good a time as any to have a look around. We just got back. I went south along the river. Nothing down there."

"I didn't find anything either," Panola said. "Not a thing but some marshy, wet country."

"That seems to be the consensus," Winkler agreed. "Nothing around."

"I wouldn't say that," Turk said slowly. Was there a traitor in the crowd? There was no telling—now. They had each gone a separate way. "I found plenty!"

Winkler got up, frowning. "You found something? What?"

"The tracks of a patrol plane—a fighter. Evidently this region is carefully patrolled. The plane lands over in a little plain across the ridge. It has landed there more than once."

"How could you tell that?" Panola demanded.

"By the tracks. Also by the ends of the sticks used to make a fire. A good woodsman," he added, and he knew if there was a guilty man here he would sense added meaning in what he said, "can read a lot of things where the average man can see nothing."

Turk Madden sat down suddenly. He was mad all through. Maybe one of them had taken a shot at him, but if he had, there was no way to prove it. He would just have to wait. He felt the weight of the .45 automatic in his shoulder holster, and liked the feel of it.

Winkler stared thoughtfully into the fire. "So they are patrolling the coast? That means we've got to go very slow."

"Well," Panola suggested, "the attack comes off in three days. When the plane comes back, let's knock him off. It would be at least two days before they'd be able to get down to investigate, and by that time, we'd be gone."

"Why two days?" Runnels asked. "They might have a radio on that ship. Probably have, in fact."

"Even so, I doubt if there would be any search organized for a couple of days. You know how bad the storms are down here. It would be all too easy for a plane to get caught in one of those terrific blasts of wind."

"It won't do," Winkler said. "We've got to keep out of sight."

"That's right," Runnels said. "Our job is not to bother with these fellows. We're to get our information and get out, and if we can do it without them having even a suspicion, so much the better."

"Well, the first thing will be for nobody to do any wandering about," Winkler said. "If we do, we'll be seen. So everybody sticks to this side of the ridge and keeps under the trees. We've got the plane camouflaged, so that won't have to be worried about."

That made sense. And yet? Suppose Winkler was the one? Suppose it was also a method of keeping them from finding anything more? And what about Panola?

"As though we were at the end of the world here," Runnels remarked. "Everything still as death except for that wind. A man would starve to death if lost on this shore."

"Yeah, and we're not so far as the crow flies from Buenos Aires. And what a town that is!"

"Have you been there?" Turk asked. "I thought I was the only one who knew South America."

"Been there?" Panola grinned. "Shucks, man, I lived there for three years! Runnels has been here, too! Weren't you here during the war?"

"Uh-huh. I was on duty as military attaché for a couple of months."

Turk ate in silence. So Panola and Runnels had both been to the Argentine? It was easy to be influenced by all that wealth and glitter. The sixteen families or so that dictated the life in the Argentine could entertain very beautifully. Perhaps one, or both, of the two men had been influenced? Persuaded?

Morning came, and he went down to the ship. Shan Bao joined him after a few minutes. He looked thoughtfully at the Manchu, then glanced around to make sure no one heard him.

"You keep your eyes open, Shan," he said softly. "You savvy? You watch everybody. Anybody do anything wrong, you tell me."

He was working over the plane when he saw Runnels and Winkler come out of the shelter. Turk turned and swung ashore. Panola was taking some weather observations, checking his instruments atop the ridge. It was as good an idea as any.

Stepping quickly over the logs, he got to the shack. None of the men had taken their carbines, and he picked up the nearest one, that of Winkler. A quick examination showed it clean. Runnels' checked the same. Then he picked up Panola's carbine. A quick glance into the barrel.

It had been fired.

Panola.

Turk went back outside and returned to the plane, his mind rehashing everything he could remember on Panola. All of them had been checked very thoroughly by the FBI, yet something had been missed.

Panola was of Italian parentage. He had been born in Brooklyn, raised there, had gone to college, and his war record had been excellent. He knew nothing beyond that, that and the fact that Panola had lived in Buenos Aires for three years sometime during this period.

Another thing remained. How had Panola, if he was the marksman, returned to the shelter so quickly the night before? There must be another route than that over the ridge.

"I think," he said musingly, "a little trip around by plane would do more good than anything else!"

Major Winkler was coming down through the trees.

"Major," he said, when the tall, narrow-faced man had come closer, "I think I'll take a cruise around. This country needs some looking over."

"You think it's wise?" Winkler asked thoughtfully. "Well, go ahead, but be careful!"

A half hour later, when Turk taxied the ship out from under the overhanging trees and the camouflaged shelter built for the plane, Shan Bao was ashore. Madden turned the ship down the pool and, after a run, lifted it into the air, banked steeply, and swung away up the coast.

After a few minutes he lifted the plane into the mists under the clouds. As he swung back and forth up the coast, he studied the terrain below. Suddenly, he saw a house!

It was a huge, gray stone building, back of a little cove with a black sand beach. A yacht was anchored in the cove, and a motor launch was at the small wharf. Easing back on the controls, he shot the amphibian into the clouds. Out of sight.

There was a chance he had not been seen, not recognized, as at the moment he had passed over the cove the mists through which he had flown were thick.

He circled the ship higher, puzzling over the situation. That house was no more than five miles from their own base! Also, it was no more than three miles from where he had been fired upon! Could he have been wrong? Perhaps it wasn't one of his own crowd, but one of these people? And perhaps Panola was in the clear!

Turk scowled grimly and hunched his big shoulders. Then he turned the plane inland toward the Dome of St. Paul. Coming up to the mountain, he pulled back on the stick and climbed to get more altitude. He was still climbing when the fighter shot out of the clouds and came toward him with all her guns spouting flame!

Turk whipped away in a climbing turn as the fighter shot beneath him, he fell away and let go with a burst at its tail assembly. Evidently he missed, for the fighter whipped around and came back at him!

Flying like a wild man, Turk put the amphibian through everything he knew, and suddenly made a break and got away into the heavy gray clouds. It was a momentary respite only, for he knew now that he dared not let the plane return to its base. Yet in a fight with a ship of that caliber, he would have no chance.

The other pilot was obviously not used to fighting, for he had missed several good chances that no member of the Luftwaffe would have missed, or a Japanese, either. Turk swung around and dropped back toward the mountain, and then suddenly he sighted the fighter again.

They saw each other at almost the same instant, but even as they sighted each other, Turk whipped over and dived straight for the rounded top of the Dome!

And behind him, the wind screaming in its wings, came the fighter! Desperate, Turk was remembering something from his own experience, a stunt he had tried long before, in the South Pacific. He was remembering, too, that curious gap in the trees atop the Dome. Heading straight for the Dome in a wild, desperate dive, he saw tracers streaming by him, and then he whipped over and cut through that gap in the trees!

A few yards in either direction and he would have crashed into the trees, and as it was, he cleared the top of the Dome by no more than four of five feet! Then, behind him, came a crash!

He took the stick back and reached for altitude, and glanced to the rear and down. A cone of leaping flame was mounting toward the sky, and he could see something he took to be the pilot's lifeless body, lying off to one side.

Thoughtfully, he turned toward home, flying high into the heavy clouds. If they searched, and they probably would, they would find the wreckage. A cursory examination would show only that the plane had crashed, and they might accept it as an accident.

Yet, if they examined closely what wreckage there was left, and one wing, at least, had fallen clear of the flames, they might find bullet holes. Still, the chances were he had missed. For the first time in his life, he found himself hoping he had missed.

He was gliding in for a landing on the pool when he saw the path, a dim trail along the rocky edge of the brook leading from the river. A path that would be a shortcut to the house on the cove!

When Turk Madden put the plane down he was worried. He got up from the pilot's seat and swore softly. Then he slid the Colt from its shoulder holster and checked the magazine. It was ready. "I think," he said softly, "I'm going to need a gun!"

Shan Bao came out in the rubber boat and took him ashore, after which he left Shan the job of snugging the ship down and checking her.

Runnels looked up when Turk walked in, then his eyes sharpened. "What happened?"

"That fighter showed up. I tricked him into a crash on top of the Dome!" Turk spoke quietly, but even as he spoke he was trying to see all their expressions at once.

Panola wet his lips slowly. "Then they know we're here. Or they will. That doesn't leave us much chance, does it?"

"Maybe they won't know," Turk suggested.

"What would prevent them?" Winkler demanded. His long, lantern-jawed face had sharpened with worry. "My heavens, man! They aren't that dumb."

"If they actually send somebody to the top of the Dome to check, I doubt if he'll find evidence of anything except a crash. They'll think he collided with the peak in a cloud. I doubt if he has any bullet holes."

"They may check his guns," Winkler suggested. "Had you thought of that?"

"I hadn't," Turk said. "But if they do, guns often fire in flames, and I doubt if there will be much left to examine. There was gasoline over everything."

"I'd say you were lucky, mighty lucky!" Runnels said. "Great stuff, old man!"

Then he told them of the yacht and the house. They watched his face curiously, but it was Winkler who seemed most worried. He paced the room thoughtfully.

"This thing scares me," he said. "They might find us!"

It was just daylight when Turk Madden slipped from the cabin. He took his carbine, and went toward the Goose, then turned away among the trees and started for the trail that led along the creek, the trail seen from the plane.

This was it. He could sense the building up of forces around him, could sense an intangible danger. Someone in his own group, he felt sure, was a traitor. It could be Panola, and yet, it might be either of the others. Winkler had been a good leader, and Turk could understand his natural worry. The atomic explosion was to be tomorrow, and if it was to be witnessed and checked, everything must move smoothly and easily. The explosion, unless the time was changed, of which they would be informed, would be at ten in the morning.

Panola was to remain here. Winkler, Runnels, and himself would fly to the vicinity, taking advantage of the cloud cover.

Then, just before ten, the explosion. They would drop through, make their check when the explosion occurred, and get away—if possible.

He knew what was at stake. The Fascists in the Argentine were strong, and they had been increased by refugees from Germany. More than one worker with atomic science had escaped to Buenos Aires, and they had been joined by others. There were rumors of money being sent to them from the north to aid the experiments by those interested in the commercial application of atomic power.

The experiments were strictly hush hush. Even the Argentine government was supposed to know nothing about them. The presence of a North American here—well, Turk Madden knew the men he was working against.

Baron von Walrath, one of the shrewdest operatives in the former German Military Intelligence; Walther Rathow, atomic scientist and militarist; Wilhelm Messner, of the Gestapo; and Miguel Farales, of the Argentine Military Intelligence.

Yet they had seen none of these men. The patrol of the coast was apparently purely routine. The whole affair had moved so perfectly that he had become suspicious. And the next few hours would tell the story.

Hurrying, he worked along the trail, then rounding a fallen log, he saw there in the soft earth, the mark of a boot! The shape was not distinct in the moss, but the heel print was plain. It could have been made no earlier than the night before.

As he continued along the trail, Turk watched carefully, and found several more footprints, but none was distinct. Yet someone had left their camp, or the vicinity of it, and had come over this trail. Then almost at the plain where he had seen the tracks of the fighter plane, he saw a double footprint. They were apparently of the same foot, and the second one was superimposed on the first, and that second track pointed toward camp! The man had come from the camp, and returned to it!

Following the footprints, he reached the dead campfire. The man he had followed had come this far. He had waited, he had smoked several cigarettes, and then he had returned the way he had come. He had waited here—for the patrol plane!

Leaving the plain, Madden crossed by way of the woods to

the range of hills beyond, stepped through the woods carefully toward the cove. He could see the cold sea water lapping on the gravel beach, and he could hear the bump of the launch hull against the small pier.

Then he leaned forward to peer at the gray house. He leaned forward still further and put a foot out to balance himself. A branch under his foot cracked like a pistol shot, and he jerked back.

Then something struck him on the head, and as he toppled forward he heard a pistol shot ringing in his ears!

He opened his eyes and saw a hard-wood floor, then blood. His own blood. He closed his eyes against the throb of his head and tried to place himself, to remember what had happened.

"Hang it, Stock," a voice was saying in English, "why did you have to shoot the man? Couldn't you get the drop on him and bring him in?"

"That guy's Turk Madden!" another voice said. "I'd know him anywhere. If you ask me, you better kill him. You leave him alive and you're borrowin' trouble. I knew him in China, and the guy is poison."

"Thanks, pal!" Turk told himself mentally, "but I don't feel very much like poison right now."

"We've got to keep him alive!" The first voice was crisp and hard. "We must keep him alive until we know where they are. Messner was to have communicated with us as soon as they landed. They aren't far from here, we know that, and he has the patrol plane stops. One of them is sure to be close to where they will be."

"Perhaps, Baron," said a third voice, suave and smooth, "we can make Madden talk. Timeo has convincing methods."

"Not a chance!" Madden rolled over and sat up. His fingers touched his scalp gingerly. The bullet had cut a neat furrow along the right side of his head. He looked up. "Unless there's some money in it."

He glanced up at the three men. Stock would be the big man with the flat face. The man seated in the chair with the smoothly shaven face and the monocle could be no one but a

German. That would be von Walrath. And the other was Latin. Probably Farales.

"Money?" Farales leaned closer. "Why should we pay you money? You have nothing we want."

"Maybe yes, and again, maybe not." Turk swallowed. "How about a drink? I'm allergic to bullets. They make me thirsty."

At a motion from Farales, Stock poured a drink and handed it to Madden. He tossed it off, shook his head, and then got slowly to his feet. There was an empty chair, and he fell back into it.

"I'm a businessman," he said then. "I'm not in this for my health. If you guys have got a better offer, trot it out."

He was stalling for time, stalling and watching. Somehow, he had to get out of here, somehow he had to block Messner, whoever he was. Certainly, one of the three men at camp was Messner, formerly of the Gestapo. To think that such a man could be in an American unit, on such a mission. But the man was there. Turk was under no illusions about stopping him. There would be only one way now.

"Who sent you here?" von Walrath demanded. "From what office do you work?"

"Office?" Turk shrugged. He took out a cigarette and put it between his lips. "I work for Turk Madden. I'm in this for myself. I'm goin' to get all the dope I can, and sell to the highest bidder."

"The United States?" Farales asked gently. He was studying Turk through narrowed eyes. "Why should they pay? They already know."

"Do they?" Madden shrugged again. "But you may find out something they won't know. Also, they may want to know how much you know."

"And that's why you're here. To find out how much we know. That's why your government sent you here." Farales' voice was silky.

"My government?" Turk raised an eyebrow. "What is my government? I fought for China before I fought for the United States. I fought for them because they paid me well, and because I like the winning side. They were a cinch to win."

Von Walrath's eyes were cold. "Then you did not believe we Germans could win? The greatest military power on earth?"

Madden chuckled. "Why the greatest? Who did you ever

lick? Nobody I can remember except a lot of little countries who never had a war. It's like Joe Louis punching a lot of guys who ride a subway. Anybody can lick an average guy if he's got some stuff. Germany was ready for war, the other countries weren't. Germany never whipped a major power who was even half ready for war."

"No?" Von Walrath sat up stiffly. "And why did we lose this one?"

"Mainly because you never had a chance." Turk warmed to his subject. "Any war can be figured on paper before it begins. You didn't have the natural resources. You were cut off from the countries that had them. You didn't have the industry."

"Next time," von Walrath replied coolly, "we won't need it. Atomic bombs change everything."

"That's right. The smallest nation has a chance now."

"Even," Farales suggested, "Argentina."

Von Walrath stood up suddenly. "Where is your plane now?" he demanded.

"Around," Madden rested his elbows on his knees. His .45 was lying on the table not a dozen feet away. "Supposing we make a deal. You slip me a chunk of dough, and I keep my plane out of this? Your man Messner can't keep it out. I can."

"And why can't Messner keep it out?" Farales demanded.

"First place," Turk looked up from under his eyebrows. He had his feet drawn back and was on his toes now, "Because he won't try. Why hasn't he communicated with you? I'll tell you why: because he hasn't any intention of it. Because he has another deal pending."

"You lie!" von Walrath hissed furiously. "I will vouch for Messner!"

Turk chuckled. "Listen, you guys. You're not so dumb. Who will pay most to get the atomic secret now? Who wants it worst? Not as a weapon, but just to make things more equal, to give herself more confidence. I ask you: who wants it? *Soviet Russia!*"

He lighted another cigarette. "What do you think they'd pay? A hundred thousand? Yes, and maybe more. Maybe a million. If a man had the secret, he could ask plenty, and get it! What can a poverty-stricken Germany give Messner? What can even the Argentine give Messner? Would he get a million from them? From you? Not a chance! What can we give your friend Messner?"

Farales' sardonic black eyes lifted to von Walrath. "He speaks wisely, Señor. What can we give your friend Messner?"

"He lies." Von Walrath's eyes were blazing, yet Madden knew he had injected an element of doubt into the Prussian's mind. "Messner is loyal."

"Then why has he not communicated with us? He is days overdue." Farales looked at Madden. "How long have you been here?"

"We landed a week ago," he lied.

"A week, and still no word. How is this, Walrath?" Farales' voice was cold. "Four times in that week has our plane been at the prescribed places. And it cannot be far. This man walked."

"Wait until the plane comes today before you speak. Messner probably has been unable to get away."

Madden could see that the Baron was uncertain. "There will be word today."

"No," Turk said coolly, "there won't."

He had been stalling for time. Stock was across the room now, mixing a drink. No one was near the table where the gun lay.

"What do you mean?" von Walrath demanded. "What makes you so sure?"

"Simply," Turk said, this was going to be close, "because your pilot is dead, and your patrol plane crashed. It's lying up there," he pointed suddenly toward the wide window and the Dome of St. Paul, "burned to a crisp!"

As he pointed, their heads almost automatically turned, and he was out of his chair and had made three steps before Farales swung and saw him. It was too late. Turk hurled himself at the table, grabbed the automatic and swung with his back to the table. Farales' shout brought a crash from Stock as he wheeled, dropping the glass and grabbing for his gun. Turk shot him in the stomach, and then wheeling, he hurled himself, shoulder first, through the window.

It was no more than six feet to the ground. The instant he hit he flattened against the building and ran along it close to the wall until he reached the end of the house.

The shore there was high, lifting in a straight bank at least ten feet above the shelving gravel beach. He jumped off the bank to the gravel, landing on his feet, and fell back into a sitting position.

As he fell backward, he saw a man on the motor launch grab a rifle, and he blasted with the Colt from where he sat. The bullet hit the cabin of the boat and laced a white scar across its polished side. The man fell over, and then the glass crashed as the fellow thrust the rifle through a cabin port. Turk was on his feet then, but he wheeled and put two quick shots through that port, and then he was running.

He had made a dozen steps before a rifle cracked and a shot hit the rocks ahead of him and whined viciously away over the water. He zigged right, and then dodged back, and seeing a cut in the bank, dropped behind it just as several more shots struck nearby.

He paused just an instant, caught a quick breath, and then ran up the cut. Ahead of him it ended near a cliff and the forest came up to the foot of the cliff. Yet there he would have to dodge across twenty feet of open country before he could make the forest.

"That German is a shot, or I miss my guess," Turk told himself. "He'll have his sights set on that open place, and I'm a dead pigeon!"

Yet even as he reached the end of the water cut, he saw there was a deep hollow and another water drain that fell sharply away. The water that had made the deeper hole had fallen off a corner of the cliff around the shoulder. Perhaps he could get across.

A huge root thrust itself out, and sticking his gun in its holster, he jumped. It was a terrific leap, but his hands just grasped the root, and he swung with all the impetus of his leap and hurled himself at the bank opposite.

He hit it, chest first, and grabbed wildly at the edge. Dust and rock cascaded into his face, and suddenly a rifle barked, and a shot smacked into the bank right between his clutching hands!

Frightened, he gave a mighty heave and hurled himself over the edge and rolled into the woods. A bullet clipped a tree over his head, and he scrambled to his feet and floundered away in the knee deep moss. Then he saw a fallen log and, leaping atop it, he ran its length, swung by a branch to another, and ran along it.

It wasn't going to be enough to get away. He had to lose them. Yet on one side was the plain, and if pushed into the open they would cut him down in an instant. On the other side was the river.

His breath was coming in great gasps, and his lungs cried out with pain at the effort. Yet he kept on, for speed meant everything now.

He had crossed a small clearing and was entering the woods along the river when suddenly another shot rang out, and he plunged head first into the soft, yielding moss. The shot had come from in *front* of him!

Turk Madden was mad. Suddenly, something had seemed to burst inside of him. The traitor, whoever he was, was up ahead, trying to kill him.

"All right!" Madden said suddenly, savagely, "if you want it you can have it!"

He slid the Colt into his hand. Four shots left. He felt in his pocket for the extra clip. Well, they hadn't taken that! Flat in the moss, he began to worm his way through the damp green softness, gun in hand, a fierce, leaping rage within him.

He crawled, and he felt the moss thinning. Was the watcher keeping an eye on him? This guy knew a thing or two, as he was the same one who had dusted the brush so thoroughly on that first day. There was a crashing in the brush back the way he came. Wish he'd shoot some of his own men!

Another crash and then he could hear someone breathing hard. The man had stopped to stare around. Slowly, Turk gathered his knees under him, and then he straightened.

The man, a huge fellow with a blackish, greasy face, was not ten feet away!

As Turk arose, the fellow stared stupidly, then gave a gulp and jerked up the rifle. He was much too slow. Turk put a bullet through his heart, then sprang across the ten feet of space, and grabbed the man's rifle. Then, without hesitating, he threw the rifle to his shoulder and dusted the woods, firing ten shots and spacing them neatly across the forest behind him.

Then he dropped the rifle and plunged down to the gravel shore of the stream. For thirty minutes he twisted and turned in the woods, and then finally straightened out and headed for home. As he walked, he exchanged clips.

As he came up to the shelter, he found Shan Bao, a carbine in his hands, standing by the door.

"Where are the others?" Turk asked.

"Around. They all went out into the brush. Thought we might be attacked. Each one took a position." Shan Bao looked at Madden's head, and the blood. "You have had trouble," he said. "I hope you killed the man who did that."

Turk dug out a cigarette and lighted it. Then he looked at the Manchu.

"I don't know, Shan, but he's got one in the stomach he wishes he didn't have!"

Runnels came out of the woods. He looked flurried, and his eyes were narrow. He glanced at Turk's head.

"Looks like you had it tough!"

"Plenty!" Turk snapped. "Better get your gear aboard the plane. We're moving!"

"Moving?" he frowned. "Winkler won't like that. Better wait to see what he says. After all this is his show."

"Up to a point," Turk Madden replied shortly. "That happens to be my plane. Anyway, they came too close just now. They'll be back. We can't stay here."

"And why shouldn't we stay here?" It was Major Winkler. His face was hot and his eyes looked angry. "I heard what you said, Madden, and we're staying, whether you like it or not."

"No," Turk replied shortly, "we're not. At least, I'm not. I'm taking my ship and getting out. I'm going back in the hills until tomorrow, back where we'll all be safe!"

"You'll stay right here." Winkler's carbine lifted, and Turk cursed himself for a fool. "You'll stay here, and like it. Panola, tie him up! This is mutiny. I'm in command here. We're in no danger, and we'll stay right here until tomorrow."

"I don't believe the gun is necessary, Major," Runnels protested. "Madden will stay."

"You bet he'll stay!" Winkler declared sharply. "I'll personally see that he stays. Tie him!"

Runnels looked at Panola, and the Italian shrugged, then he stepped forward and jerked Turk's hands behind him. Yet even as Panola tied his hands, Turk knew the officer was not tying him tight. Was it because he sympathized or because he hoped he would try to escape, and be shot escaping?

Tied on his bed, Turk relaxed and lay quiet. How soon the Baron would find them, he couldn't guess. Obviously, it couldn't be long. The possible areas now were so limited, for they knew he had come from some place within walking distance, which meant no more than ten miles, or perhaps a bit more. It was rough, rugged country, but they would be looking.

Working a little, he loosened his ropes. Major Winkler had been lying down for several minutes now, and Runnels was sitting in the door.

Panola was nowhere in sight. Had he gone to warn von Walrath finally to make contact? Yet somehow, despite the apparently obvious evidence, Turk found himself doubting that Panola was the guilty man. But even that left only Runnels and Winkler, and Winkler was in command. He would be blamed for the success or failure of the effort.

Winkler got up suddenly and walked outside. He said something to Runnels about being nervous.

"Nothing must happen now," he muttered.

Turk lay still. His hands were free. Now where was Shan Bao? He drew his knees up and worked on the ropes on his ankles. Runnels still sat in the doorway. There was no sign of Panola or Major Winkler.

He put one foot down beside the cot, then turned carefully and sat up. Runnels had not moved. His head lay against the door post, and he was apparently asleep. Turk got up and in two quick steps had crossed the room to his carbine.

He picked up a handful of extra clips and thrust them into his pockets. He retrieved his automatic and more ammunition, then he stepped over to the back wall. In a few minutes he had worked his way through the branches and leaves of the shelter and stood outside.

A shot rang out, and he heard a muffled curse, and then he saw men come streaming into camp. He had made it none too soon. He saw Runnels start up and then go crashing down as he was struck by a gun butt. Then they charged inside, and he heard a shout as they failed to find him.

"And they knew where to look," Madden said viciously.

*   *   *

He moved swiftly through the darkness toward the cliff. He knew where he was going now. He needed shelter, and there was the cave above. He climbed swiftly, and found his way to the cave. For a while he had been afraid he would not be able to find it in the dark, but he did. Then he crawled in and lay still.

They were searching down below, and he heard the voice of von Walrath as well as that of Farales. Something had gone wrong, apparently something more than the fact that he was gone. They kept searching, then finally gave up. But they remained below. He was bottled up, unable to do a thing.

Where was Shan Bao? Had Runnels been killed? And what of the others? Unable to sit still, he turned on his flashlight, shielding it with his hand, and went to the back of the cave. It was a steep, winding passage, and he went down, walking swiftly. It took a sharp turn, and suddenly he realized it was going toward the shore of the pool!

There was dampness here, and occasional pools of water. He walked on, then feeling the air moving against his face, he proceeded more cautiously. It was a large opening, almost concealed behind a fallen log. But he was looking over the pool—and there, not a dozen feet away, was the Goose!

How far had he walked? And what was the Goose doing here?

Considering, he realized he must have walked at least twenty minutes inside the cave. He could have come a mile, but probably it was no more than half that far. In his mind he ran his eyes along the edge of the pool. Then he knew. Somehow, some way, the Goose had been slipped away and hidden in this inlet at the extreme end of the pool.

It was only a delay, for with daylight they would find it with ease. And by daylight the Goose should be winging out to sea instead of lying here.

He crawled over the log, then moved ahead slowly, carefully. He was going to be aboard that plane or dead within the next few minutes. Suddenly, right ahead of him, something moved.

Turk froze. Then he saw a tall, lean form rise before him. Instantly, he grinned with relief. Shan Bao!

"Shan!" he whispered hoarsely, and saw the figure stiffen. Then the Manchu turned and beckoned.

"What is it?" Madden whispered as he came up. "How'd the plane get here!"

"Panola," Shan replied softly. "Panola and me."

"Panola?" Madden scowled. Then Panola wasn't the one. Crawling out along a log to the door of the ship, he puzzled over that. Then he slipped in. The Italian moved, and touched his arm.

"Madden? Man, I'm glad you're here! I can't fly this thing good enough. We towed her down here with the rubber boat. Maybe we can take off."

"We can!" Turk shifted his carbine. "Panola, who's the traitor, Runnels or Winkler?"

"I don't know," he shrugged. "You mean one of them isn't on the level?"

"That's right. And I thought it was you! You, because of your rifle. Somebody fired on me that first day, and your rifle was the only one fired that day."

Panola grabbed his arm.

"But Turk!" he said hoarsely. "I didn't have my own gun that day. I got another by mistake. Major Winkler had mine!"

"Major Winkler?" Turk's jaw set. "Then Winkler is Wilhelm Messner, the Gestapo agent!"

He turned sharply. "Panola, you stay with this ship. Stay with it and don't let anybody aboard but Shan or me. I'm going ashore."

"But what can you do?" Panola protested. "Only two of you?"

"Watch!" Turk snapped harshly. "Shan is worth a dozen. Watch, and you'll see how it's done. This isn't cricket, but it's business!"

He walked back to the gun case and took out a submachine gun, and slid in a magazine. He thrust three more in his belt. Then he went ashore. He went through the woods fast with Shan, also armed with a submachine gun, following close behind.

There was no effort at concealment when he stepped up toward the shelter. His very carelessness made the guard relax. Turk stepped out of the brush and saw the guard suddenly stiffen. Then he let out a low cry and grabbed for his gun.

He never made it. Turk opened up with the tommy and cut him half in two with the first blast of fire. Men scrambled to their feet and the two men mowed them down. Leaping into the open, Turk felt a gun blast almost in his face, and then he shoved the tommy against the big man who lunged at him and opened up.

The Baron charged from a door, gun spouting, and Turk
Madden cut down on him and saw the blasting lead of the
tommy almost smash his head to bits. The man went flat and
rolled over, grabbing feebly at the earth, his hands helpless,
his gun rattling on the rocks.

Then someone leaped from the shambles and made a dart for
the outer darkness. It was Winkler!

Dropping his tommy gun, Turk sprang after him. Plunging
wildly through the brush, the man charged at the cliff and
began a mad scramble up its surface with Turk close behind
him.

They met at the top, and Winkler, his features wolfish with
fury, whirled to face him. He aimed a vicious kick at Turk's
face as he came over the edge, but Turk ducked and grabbed
his foot. His hold slipped, but it was enough to stagger Messner,
and before the Gestapo man could get set, Turk Madden was
on top.

In the darkness there on the brink of the cliff, they fought.
Turk, sweating from his climb, leaped in for a kill, and Messner,
like a tiger at bay, struck out. His fist smashed Turk in the
mouth, and Madden felt his lips smash and tasted blood, and
something deep within him awakened and turned him utterly
vicious. Toe to toe, the two big men slugged like madmen.
There was no back step, no hesitation, no ducking or dodging.
It was cruel and bitter and brutal. It was primeval in its fury.

Turk went down, and then he came up swinging, and Messner,
triumph shining in his ugly eyes, smashed him down again and
leaped in to put the boots to him. Turk rolled over and scrambled up, smashing Messner in the stomach with a wicked butt.

Staggering, the German couldn't get set before the furious
onslaught of those iron fists. His face streaming blood, his nose
a pulp where the bone had been crushed, he backed and
backed.

Relentless, ruthless, Turk closed in. He ducked a left and
smashed a wicked right to the body. He felt the wind go out of
the German, and he stepped in, hooking both hands to the
head and then the body. He caught a long swing on his ear that
made his head ring, but he was beyond pain, beyond fear,
beyond doubt.

It was a fight to the death now, and he fought. He stepped under another swing and battered at the German's body with cruel punches. Then he straightened and whipped up a right uppercut that jerked the German's head back. Then a crushing left hook, and as the German went to his knees he smashed him again in the face.

The man fell back and then rolled over and got up. Turk started for him, and the man turned, gave a despairing cry, and sprang straight out from the cliff!

It was a sheer drop to the jagged rocks and upthrust roots and jagged dead branches below.

Turk stepped back, his chest heaving with effort, his eyes blind with sweat and blood. Then he turned, and slowly and with effort he walked back to the path and went down to the shelter.

Runnels met him, a tommy gun in his hands.

"Get him?" he asked.

Turk nodded. "Yeah." He glanced toward the east where the sky was beginning to lighten. "Shan, fix some coffee. Then we'll get the ship warmed up. We've got us a job to do."

"Madden," Panola said slowly, "I did some looking around myself. Rathow, the atomic scientist, and Miguel Farales are back at the house. The bomb that is to be dropped is there. One of them, anyway."

"You saw it?" Turk exclaimed, increduously.

"I wired it," Panola said, grinning. "I wired the blasted thing." He added, then, "The other comes over the house about nine. It will be in a big bomber and guarded by a fighter plane. There will be another plane, a big passenger job, of scientists."

"Then that's our job!" Turk said. "We've got to get the fighter. If we can knock out the fighter, the others are sitting pigeons." He turned to Panola. "How'd you wire that bomb?"

"The first person who slams the door on the back of the house will blow that whole cove into the mist," Panola replied grimly. "It isn't more than half the size of our Hiroshima bomb, though."

When Madden's amphibian took off, all were aboard. Turk Madden scowled at the sky, and his hard green eyes searched the horizon for the oncoming planes. They should be along soon. He reached for altitude and squeezed the Goose against the low hanging clouds.

Getting a fighter was anything but simple, and he knew there was every chance it would end in failure. Of course, he could go ahead, observe the experiment, and return so they could report their findings.

Yet, if all could be destroyed, the experimenters who remained in Buenos Aires would be unsure of just what had happened and where the mistake had been made. It would certainly slow up experimentation and increase uncertainty and fear.

Shan Bao saw them first. The Manchu leaned over and touched Turk on the shoulder and gestured.

The bomber was flying at about six thousand feet, with the passenger plane and its observers on the right and a bit behind. For a moment the fighter eluded him, and then he saw it high against the sky, flying at probably nine thousand, his own level. He eased back on the stick and climbed, hoping with all his heart that the fighter pilot had not sighted him.

It would be touch and go now. There would be no such chance as with the other fighter, a few days before. He could not hope for such a thing twice. Even the maneuver was risky, and the chance of the pilot making a mistake was slight. The man in this ship would probably be tough and experienced. He had one chance in a million, and only one, that was to dive out of the clouds and get a burst into the fighter before he realized what had happened.

They were a good eight or ten miles from the house on the cove now. He leveled off at eleven thousand, thankful it wasn't as heavily overcast as usual, and watched the planes below him.

Suddenly, the Goose seemed to jump in the air. Startled, he looked at his instruments, and then a rolling wave of sound hit him and he jerked his head as if struck, and at the same time the ship rolled heavily.

"Look!" Panola screamed, and following his outthrust arm and finger, they saw a gigantic column of smoke and debris lifting toward the sky!

"Somebody slammed a door!" Runnels said grimly.

Turk was jolted momentarily, and then suddenly, he saw his chance!

"Hold everything!" he yelled, and swung the ship over into a screaming dive.

The fighter had been jolted, too, and the ships ahead were wavering. In the picture that flashed through his mind, Turk could see their doubt, their hesitation.

Something had happened. What? The bomb at the house had gone up, but how? Why? And their own bomber was carrying another bomb. Would there be enough radio activity at this distance to affect it? Who among them knew? After all, this was a new explosive, and how volatile it was, they could not guess. And what had caused the other explosion? Might this one go, too?

The fighter pilot must have sensed something, or his roving eyes must have caught a glimpse of the plane shooting down on his tail. In a sudden, desperate effort, he pulled his fighter into a climbing turn, and it was the wrong thing.

Turk opened up with all his guns. Saw his tracers stream into the fighter's tail, saw the pursuit ship fall away, and then banking steeply, he sent a stream of tracer and steel, stabbing at the fighter's vitals like a white hot blade!

There was a sudden puff of smoke, a desperate effort as the fighter flopped over once and fired a final, despairing burst that streamed uselessly off into space. Then it rolled upside down and, sheathed in flame, went screaming away down the thousands of feet toward the crags below.

The other ships must have seen the fighter go, for they split apart at once. One flying north, the other south. With a gleam in his eyes, Turk saw it was the bomber that turned south. "We got 'em," he yelled. "This is the payoff!"

Runnels, his face deathly pale, touched his shoulder.

"Turk!" he yelled. "If you hit that bomb, we're done for!"

"Wait, and watch!" Madden yelled. He rolled over and went streaking after the passenger ship. His greater speed brought him up fast, and he could see the other plane fighting desperately to get away.

In that passenger plane would be the men who knew, the men whose knowledge of atomic power could give the militarists of the world a terrible weapon, a weapon to bring chaos to the world. It was like shooting a sitting duck, but he had to do it. His face set and his jaw hard, he opened the Goose up and let it have everything it had left.

Swiftly he overhauled the passenger plane, which dived desperately to escape. It came closer to the hills below, and Turk swung closer. He glanced at the gigantic Dome of St. Paul, coming closer now, and then he did a vertical bank, swung around and went roaring at the plane!

The pilot was game. He made a desperate effort, and then the probing fingers of Turk's tracer stabbed into his tail assembly. The ship swung off her course, lost altitude, and the pilot tried to bank away from the rounded peak of the Dome. He tried too late. With a terrific crash and a gigantic burst of flame, the passenger plane crashed belly first against the mountain side.

For an instant the flaming wreck clung to the steep side, then it sagged, something gave way, and like a flaming arrow it plunged into the deep canyon below.

Turk shook himself, and his face relaxed a little, then he started climbing.

"Two down," he said aloud, "and one to go!"

He went into a climbing turn. Up, up, up. Far off to the south he could see the plane bearing the atomic bomb, a mere speck against the sky now.

It was an old type plane, with a cruising speed of no more than a hundred and fifty miles per hour. With his ship he could beat that by enough. For the fiftieth time he thanked all the gods that he was lucky enough to have picked up this experimental model with its exceptional speed. He leveled off and opened the ship up.

Runnels had moved up into the copilot's seat. He glanced at Turk, but said nothing. His face was white and strained. Behind him, Turk could hear Panola breathing with deep sighs. Only Shan Bao seemed unchanged, phlegmatic.

As the lean Manchu thrust his head lower for better vision, Turk glimpsed his hawklike yellow face and the gleam in his eye. It was such a face as the Mongol raiders of the khans must have had, the face of a hunter, the face of a fighter. There was in that face no recognition of consequences, only the desperate eagerness to close with the enemy, to fight, to win.

Turk's eyes were cold now. He knew what he had to do. That atomic bomb must go. No such power could be left in the hands of these power-mad, force-minded men. It must go. If his own plane and all in it had to go, the cost would be slightly balanced against the great saving to civilization and the world of people. Yet that sacrifice might not be necessary. He had a plan.

He swung his ship inland for several miles, flying a diagonal course that carried him south and west. The bomber was still holding south, intent only on putting distance between them.

Turk knew what that pilot was thinking. He was thinking of the awful force he carried with him, of what would happen if they were machine-gunned or forced to crash-land. That pilot was afraid. He wanted distance, freedom from fear.

Yet Turk was wondering if the pilot could see what was happening. Did that other flyer guess what was in his mind? And Turk was gaining, slowly, steadily gaining, drawing up on the bomber. It was still a long way ahead. But it was over Canal Ladrillero now, and as Turk moved up to the landward, the bomber followed the canal southwest.

Deliberately, Turk cut his speed back to one hundred and fifty. Runnels glanced at him, puzzled, but Turk held his course, and said nothing. At the last minute, the enemy pilot seemed to realize what was happening and made a desperate effort to change course, but Turk moved up, and the bomber straightened out once again.

There was one thing to watch for. One thing that might get the bomber away. He would think of that soon, Turk realized. And that would be the instant of greatest danger.

"Watch!" he said suddenly. "If he drops that bomb, yell! That's his only chance now."

Runnels jumped suddenly as the idea hit him.

"Why! Why, you're herding him out to sea," he shouted. "You're herding him out there where his bomb won't do any damage!"

"Yeah," Madden nodded grimly, "and where he won't have gas enough to get back."

"What about us?" Panola asked.

"Us?" Turk shrugged. "I think we've got more gas than he has. He wasn't expecting this. We had enough to fly us back to our mother ship. If we have to, we can sit down on the water and last awhile. This is a boat, you know. We could probably last long enough in this sea so that the ship could come up with us. We'll radio as soon as we get this bomber out far enough."

They were over two hundred miles out, and still herding the bomber before Runnels let out a yell. But Turk had seen the bomber jump and had seen the bomb fall away.

He whipped the ship over into a steep climbing turn and went away from there fast. Even so, the concussion struck them with a terrific blow, and the plane staggered, and then he looked back at the huge column of water mounting into the sky, and then the awful roar as thousands upon thousands of tons of water geysered up and tumbled back into the sea.

Turk banked again, searching for the bomber. It was there, still farther out to sea, and Turk turned again and started after him.

"All right, Panola," he said. "In code, call our own ship. I hope they survived the tidal wave caused by that bomb."

The bomber was farther out now, and they moved after him, and in a moment, Panola leaned over.

"She's all right. About two hundred miles north and west."

Turk turned the amphibian, keeping the bomber in view, but angling away. "He may reach land," he said over his shoulder. "But if he does he'll crash on the coast of Chile. He'll never make it back to the Argentine!"

Runnels leaned back and ran his finger around inside of his collar.

"For a while you had me worried," he said grimly. "I thought you were going to tangle with that bomb!"

Turk chuckled. "Not me, buddy! I'm saving this lily white body of mine for the one and only girl!"

'Yeah?" Runnels was skeptical. "And you've got a girl in every port?"

"Not me. I haven't been in every port!"

AUTHOR'S NOTE
Wings Over Khabarovsk

This is the first story I wrote about Siberia, the forbidding frontier I explore in much greater detail in my novel Last of the Breed.

The first person to tell me about Siberia in detail was One-Armed Sutton, the legendary adventurer who was one of several inspirations for Turk Madden. Sutton was a Canadian, if I recall correctly, who'd gone to Siberia to try to get his hands on some of the gold bars the White Russians had brought from the motherland. He also did some gold dredging on a river there, but I think the natives decided he was doing too well and shut him down.

He had worked with a half-dozen warlords in China before that, at different times, and built mortars for them. Somewhere along the line he lost his arm.

He and his stories meant a lot to me.

WINGS OVER KHABAROVSK

The drone of the two radial motors broke the still white silence. As far as the eye could reach the snow-covered ridges of the Sihote Alin Mountains showed no sign of life. Turk Madden banked the Grumman and studied the broken terrain below. It was remote and lonely, this range along the Siberian coast.

He swung his ship in a slow circle. That was odd. A half dozen fir trees had no snow on their branches.

He leveled off and looked around, then saw what he wanted, a little park, open and snow-covered, among the trees. It was just the right size, by the look of it. He'd chance the landing. He slid down over the treetops, setting the ship down with just barely enough room. Madden turned the ship before he cut the motor.

Taking down a rifle, he kicked his feet into snowshoes and stepped out into the snow. It was almost spring in Siberia, but the air was crisp and cold. Far to the south, the roads were sodden with melting snow, and the rivers swollen with spring floods. War would be going full blast again soon.

He was an hour getting to the spot. Even before he reached it, his eyes caught the bright gleam of metal. The plane had plunged into the fir trees, burying its nose in the mountainside. In passing, it had knocked the snow from the surrounding trees, and there had been no snow for several days now. That was sheer luck. Ordinarily it would have snowed, and the plane would have been lost beyond discovery in these lonely peaks.

* * *

163

Not a dozen feet from the tangled wreckage of the ship he could see a dark bundle he knew instinctively was the flyer. Lutvin had been his friend. The boyish young Russian had been a great favorite at Khabarovsk Airport. Suddenly, Turk stopped.

Erratic footprints led from the crashed plane to the fallen body. Lutvin had been alive after the crash!

Madden rushed forward and turned the body over. His wild hope that the boy might still be alive died instantly. The snow under the body was stained with blood. Fyodor Lutvin had been machine-gunned as he ran from his fallen plane.

Machine-gunned! But that meant—

Turk Madden got up slowly, and his face was hard. He turned toward the wreckage of the plane, began a slow, painstaking examination. What he saw convinced him. Fyodor Lutvin had been shot down, then, after his plane had crashed, had been ruthlessly machine-gunned by his attacker.

But why? And by whom? It was miles from any known front. The closest fighting was around Murmansk, far to the west. Only Japan, lying beyond the narrow strip of sea at Sakhalin and Hokkaido. And Japan and Russia were playing a game of mutual hands off. But Lutvin had been shot down and then killed. His killers had wanted him dead beyond question.

There could be only one reason—because he knew something that must not be told. The fierce loyalty of the young flyer was too well known to be questioned, so he must have been slain by enemies of his country.

Turk Madden began a systematic search, first of the body, then of the wreckage. He found nothing.

Then he saw the camera. Something about it puzzled him. He studied it thoughtfully. It was smashed, yet—

Then he saw. The camera was smashed, but it had been smashed after it had been taken apart—*after the film had been removed*. Where then, was the film?

He found it a dozen feet away from the body, lying in the snow. The film was in a waterproof container. Studying the situation, Turk could picture the scene.

Lutvin had photographed something. He had been pursued, shot down, but had lived through the crash. Scrambling from the wrecked ship with the film, he had run for shelter in the rocks. Then, as he tumbled under the hail of machine-gun fire, he had thrown the film from him.

Turk Madden took the film and, picking up his rifle, started up the steep mountainside toward the park where he had left the Grumman. He was just stepping from a clump of fir when a shot rang out. The bullet smacked a tree trunk beside him and stung his face with bits of bark.

Turk dropped to his hands and knees and slid back into the trees. Ahead of him, and above him, was a bunch of boulders. Even as he looked a puff of smoke showed from the boulders, and another shot rang out. The bullet clipped a twig over his head. Madden fired instantly, coolly pinking every crevice and crack in the boulders. He did not hurry.

His final shot sounded, and instantly he was running through the soft snow. He made it to a huge fir a dozen feet away before the rifle above him spoke. He turned and fired again.

Indian-fashion, he circled the clump of boulders. But when he was within sight of them, there was no one about. For a half hour he waited, then slid down. On the snow in the center of the rocks, he found two old cartridge cases. He studied them.

"Well, I'll be blowed! A Berdianka!" he muttered. "I didn't think there was one outside a museum!"

The man's trail was plain. He wore moccasins made of fur, called *unty*. One of them was wrapped in a bit of rawhide, apparently.

His rifle was ready, Turk fell in behind. But after a few minutes it became obvious that his attacker wanted no more of it. Outgunned, the man was making a quick retreat. After a few miles, Madden gave up and made his way slowly back to his own ship. The chances were the man had been sent to burn the plane, to be sure a clean job had been made of the killing. But that he was wearing *unty* proved him no white man, and no Japanese either, but one of the native Siberian tribes.

It was after sundown when Turk Madden slid into a long glide for the port of Khabarovsk. In his coat pocket the film was heavy. He was confident that it held the secret of Lutvin's death.

There was a light in Commissar Chevski's office. Turk hesitated, then slipped off his helmet and walked across the field toward the shack. A dark figure rose up from the corner of the hangar, and a tall, stooped man stepped out.

"Shan Bao!" Madden said. "Take care of the ship, will you?"

The Manchu nodded, his dark eyes narrow.

"Yes, comrade." He hesitated. "The commissar asking for you. He seem angry."

"Yeah?" Madden shrugged. "Thanks. I'll see him." He walked on toward the shack without a backward glance. Shan Bao could be trusted with the plane. Where the tall Manchu had learned the trade, Turk could not guess, but the man was a superb plane mechanic. Since Madden's arrival from the East Indies, he had attached himself to Turk and his Grumman, and the ship was always serviced and ready.

Turk tapped lightly on Chevski's door, and at the word walked in.

Commissar Chevski was a man with a reputation for efficiency. He looked up now, his yellow face crisp and cold. The skin was drawn tightly over his cheekbones, his long eyes almost as yellow as his face. He sat behind his table staring at Turk inscrutably. Twice only had Turk talked with him. Around the port the man had a reputation for fierce loyalty and driving ambition. He worked hard and worked everyone else.

"Comrade Madden," he said sharply. "You were flying toward the coast today! Russia is at war with Germany, and planes along the coast invite trouble with Japan. I have given orders that there shall be no flying in that direction!"

"I was ordered to look for Comrade Lutvin," Madden said mildly, "so I flew over the Sihote Atlins."

"There was no need," Chevski's voice was sharp. "Lutvin did not fly in that direction."

"You're mistaken," Turk said quietly, "I found him."

Chevski's eyes narrowed slightly. He leaned forward intently. "You found Lutvin? Where?"

"On a mountainside in the Sihote Atlins. His plane had crashed. He was dead. His ship had been shot down from behind, and Comrade Lutvin had been machine-gunned as he tried to escape the wreck."

Chevski stood up.

"What is this nonsense?" he demanded. "Who would machine-gun a Russian flyer on duty? We have no enemies here."

"What about Japan?" Madden suggested. "But that need make no difference. The facts are as I say. Lutvin was shot down—then killed."

"You *landed*?" Chevski demanded. He walked around from behind his desk. He shook his head impatiently. "I am sorry, comrade. I spoke hastily. This is serious business, very serious. It means sabotage, possibly war on a new front."

Chevski walked back behind the table. He looked up suddenly.

"Comrade Madden, I trust you will say nothing of this to anyone until I give the word. This is a task for the OGPU, you understand?"

Madden nodded, reaching toward his pocket. "But, com—"

The Russian lifted a hand.

"Enough. I am busy. You have done a good day's work. Report to me at ten tomorrow. Good night." He sat down abruptly and began writing vigorously.

Turk hesitated, thinking of the film. Then, shrugging, he went out and closed the door.

Hurrying to his own quarters, he gathered his materials and developed the film. Then he sat down and began studying the pictures. For hours, he sat over them, but could find nothing. The pictures were of a stretch of Siberian coast near the mouth of the Nahtohu River. They were that, and no more. Finally, almost at daylight, he gave up and fell into bed.

It was hours later when he awakened. For an instant he lay on his back staring upward, then glanced at his wristwatch. Nine-thirty. He would have barely time to shave and get to Chevski's office. He rolled over and sat up. Instantly, he froze. The pictures, left on the table, were gone!

Turk Madden sat very still. Slowly, he studied the room. Nothing had been taken except the pictures, the film, and the can in which it had been carried. He crossed the room and examined the door and window. The latter was still locked, bore no signs of having been opened. The door was as he had left it the night before. On the floor, just inside the door, was the fading print of a damp foot.

Madden dressed hurriedly and strapped on a gun. Then he went outside. The snow was packed hard, but when he stepped to the corner he saw a footprint. The snow was melting, and already there were three dark lines of earth showing across the track under his window, three lines that might have been made by an *unty* with a rawhide thong around it!

Suddenly, Turk glanced up. A squad of soldiers was coming toward him on the double. They halted before him, and their officer spoke sharply.

"Comrade Madden! You are under arrest!"

"Me?" Turk gasped, incredulous. "What for?"

"Come with us. You will know in good time."

They took him at once to Commissar Chevski's office. Turk was led in and stopped before Chevski's desk. There were five other men in the room. Colonel Granatman sat at the table beside Chevski. In a corner sat Arseniev of the Intelligence. He looked very boyish except for his eyes. They were hard and watchful. The other two men Madden did not know.

"Comrade Madden!" Granatman demanded. "You flew yesterday over the Sihote Atlin Mountains? You did this without orders?"

"Yes, but—"

"The prisoner," Chevski said coldly, "will confine himself to replies to questions."

"You reported that you found there the body of Comrade Fyodor Lutvin, is that right?"

"Yes." Turk was watching the proceedings with astonishment. What was this all about?

"What are the caliber of the guns on your ship?" Granatman asked. "Fifty caliber, are they not?"

"Yes."

"Comrade Olentiev," Granatman said, "tell us what you found when Commissar Chevski sent you to investigate."

Olentiev stepped forward, clicking his heels. He was a short, powerful man with a thick neck and big hands. He was, Madden knew, an agent of the OGPU, the all-powerful secret police.

"I found Fyodor Lutvin had been shot through the body with fifteen fifty-caliber bullets. His plane had been shot down. The gas tank was riddled, feedline broken, and instrument panel smashed. Most of the controls were shot away.

"I found the tracks of a man and where he had turned the

body over, and followed those tracks to where a plane had been landed in the mountains nearby.

"On return I reported to Commissar Chevski, then received the report of my assistant, Blavatski. He ascertained that on the night of Thursday last, Comrade Lutvin won three hundred rubles from Comrade Madden at dice."

"Commissar Chevski," Granatman asked slowly, "who in your belief could have attacked Lutvin in that area?"

"The colonel is well aware," Chevski said quietly, "that Russia is at war only with Germany. If we have a killing here, it is my belief it is murder!"

"Colonel Granatman," Turk protested, "there was evidence of another sort. I found near the body a can containing aerial photographs taken along the coast near the mouth of the Nahtohu River."

"Photographs?" Granatman frowned. "Did you report them to the commissar?"

"No, I—"

"You developed them yourself?" Granatman interrupted. "Where are they?"

"They were stolen from my quarters last night," Madden said.

"Ah!" Chevski said. "You had photographs but they were stolen. You did not report them last night. You flew over a forbidden area, and you, of all those who looked, knew where to find Fyodor Lutvin's body!"

Granatman frowned.

"I would like to believe you innocent, Comrade Madden. You have done good work for us, but there seems no alternative."

Turk Madden stared in consternation. Events had moved so rapidly he could scarcely adjust himself to the sudden and complete change in affairs. The matter of the three hundred rubles had been nothing, and he had promptly forgotten it. A mere sixty dollars or so was nothing. In Shanghai he had often lost that many hundreds, and won as much.

"Say, what is this?" Turk demanded. "I'm sent out to look for a lost plane, I find it, and then you railroad me! Whose toes have I been stepping on around here?"

"You will have a fair trial, comrade," Granatman assured him. "This is just a preliminary hearing. Until then you will be held."

Olentiev and Blavatski stepped up on either side of him, and
he was marched off without another word. His face grim, he
kept still. There was nothing he could do now. He had to admit
there was a case, if a flimsy one. That he had gone right to the
body, when it was where it wasn't expected to be—that there
was no other known plane in the vicinty but his own—that the
gun calibers were identical—that he had landed and examined
the body—that money had been won from him by Lutvin—
that he had told an unverified story of stolen photographs.

Through it all, Arseniev had said nothing. And Arseniev was
supposed to be his friend! The thought was still puzzling him
when he became conscious of the drumming of a motor. Looking to the runway, not sixty feet away, he saw a small pursuit
ship. The motor was running, it had been running several
minutes, and no one was anywhere near.

He glanced around quickly. There was no one in sight. His
captors were at least a dozen feet away and appeared to be
paying no attention. Their guns were buttoned under their
tunics. It was the chance of a lifetime. He took another quick
glance around, set himself for a dash to the plane. Then his
muscles relaxed under a hammering suspicion.

It was too easy. The scene was too perfect. There wasn't a
flaw in this picture anywhere. Deliberately, he stopped, waiting for his guards to catch up. As he half-turned, waiting, he
saw a rifle muzzle projecting just beyond the corner of a building. Even as he looked, it was withdrawn.

He broke into a cold sweat. He would have been dead
before he'd covered a dozen feet! Someone was out to get him.
But who? And why?

The attitude of his captors changed suddenly, they dropped
their careless manner, and came up alongside.

"Quick!" Olentiev snapped. "You loafer. You murderer. We'll
show you. A firing squad you'll get for what you did to Lutvin!"

Turk Madden said nothing. He was taken to the prison and
shoved into a cell. The room was of stone, damp and chilly.
There was straw on the floor, and a dirty blanket. Above him,
on the ground level, was a small, barred window.

He looked around bitterly.

"Looks like you're behind the eightball, pal!" he told himself. "Framed for a murder, and before they get through, you'll be stuck."

He walked swiftly across the cell, leaped, and seized the bars. They were strong, thicker than they looked. A glance at the way they were set into the concrete told him there was no chance there. He lay down on the straw and tried to think. Closing his eyes, he let his mind wander back over the pictures. Something. There had been something there. If he only knew!

But although the pictures were clear in his mind, he could remember nothing. Thinking of that lonely stretch of coast brought another picture to his mind. Before his trip to pick up Arseniev from the coast of Japan he had consulted charts of both coasts carefully. There was something wrong in his mind. Something about his memory of the chart of the coast and the picture of the coast near the Nahtohu River didn't click.

The day passed slowly. The prison sat near the edge of a wash or gully on the outskirts of town. The bank behind the prison, he had noticed, was crumbling. If he could loosen one of the floor-stones—it was only a chance, but that was all he asked.

Shadows lengthened in the cell, then it was dark, although the light through the window was still gray. Pulling back the straw, he found the outline of a stone block.

The prison was an old building, put together many years ago, still with a look of seasoned strength. Yet time and the elements had taken their toll. Water had run in through the ground-level window, and it had drained out through a hole on the low side. But in running off, it had found the line of least resistance along the crack in the floor. Using the broken spoon with which he was to eat, he began to work at the cement. It crumbled easily, but the stone of the floor was thick.

Four hours passed before he gave up. He had cut down over three inches all around, but still the block was firm, and the handle of his spoon would no longer reach far enough. For a long time he lay still, resting and thinking. Outside all was still, yet he felt restless. Someone about the airport wanted him dead. Someone here was communicating with the man who wore the *unty*, who had fired at him with the old Berdianka in the mountains. Whoever that person was would not rest until, he, Turk Madden, was killed.

That person would have access to this prison, and if he were killed, in the confusion of war, not too much attention would be paid. Arseniev had been his only real friend here, and Arseniev had sat quietly and said nothing. Chevski was efficiency personified. He was interested only in the successful functioning of the port.

But it was more than his own life that mattered. Here, at this key port, close to the line that carried supplies from Vladivostok to the western front, an enemy agent could do untold damage. Lutvin had discovered something, had become suspicious. Flying to the coast, he had photographed something the agent did not want known. Well, what?

At least, if he could not escape, he could think. What would there be on the coast that a man could photograph? A ship could be moved, so it must be some permanent construction. An airport? Turk sat up restlessly. Thinking was all right, but action was his line. He sat back against the wall and stared at the block of stone. The crack was wide. Suddenly, he forced both heels into the crack, and, bracing himself against the wall, pushed.

The veins swelled in his forehead, his palms pressed hard against the floor, but he shoved, and shoved hard. Something gave, but it was not the block against which he pushed. It was the wall behind him. He struggled to his feet, and turned. It was much too dark to see, but he could feel.

His fingers found the cracks in the stones, and his heart gave a great leap. The old wall was falling apart, the cheap cement crumbling. What looked so strong was obviously weak. The prison had been thrown together by convict labor eighty years before, or so he had been told. He seized his spoon and went to work.

In a moment, he had loosened a block. He lifted it out and placed it on the floor beside him. What lay beyond? Another cell? He shrugged. At least he was busy. He took down another block, another, and then a fourth. He crawled through the hole, then carefully, shielding it with his hands, struck a match.

His heart sank. He was in a cell, no different from his own. He rose to his feet and tiptoed across to the door. He took the iron ring in his hand and turned. It moved easily, and the door swung open!

A faint movement in the shadowy hall outside stopped him. Carefully, he moved himself into the doorway, and glanced along the wall.

He caught his breath. A dark figure crouched before his own door and, slowly, carefully, opened it!

Like a shadow, the man straightened, and his hand slipped into his shirt front, coming out with a long knife. Turk's eyes narrowed. In two quick steps he was behind the man. There must have been a sound, for the man turned, catlike. Turk Madden's fist exploded on the corner of the man's jaw like a six-inch shell, and the fellow crumpled. Madden stepped in, hooking viciously to the short ribs. He wet his lips. "That'll hold you, pal," he muttered.

Stooping, he retrieved the knife. Then he frisked the man carefully, grinned when he found a Luger automatic and several clips of cartridges. He pocketed them, then turned the man over. He was a stranger. Carefully, noticing signs of returning consciousness, he bound and gagged the man, then closed the cell door on him, and locked it. Returning to the cell from which he had escaped, he put the stones back into place, then put the key out of sight on a stone ledge above the door.

Turning, he walked down the hall. The back door was not locked, and he went out into the night. For an instant, he stood still. He was wondering about his own ship. He knew what there was to do. He had to fly to the coast and see for himself. He thought he knew what was wrong, but on the other hand—

Also, there was the business of Lutvin's killer. He had flown a plane. He might still be there, and if he saw the Grumman—

Turk Madden smiled grimly. He crossed the open spaces toward the hangars, walking swiftly. Subterfuge wouldn't help. If he tried slipping around he would surely be seen. The direct approach was best. A sleepy sentry stared at him, but said nothing. Turk opened the small door and walked in.

Instantly, he faded back into the shadows inside the door. Not ten feet away Commissar Chevski was staring at Shan Bao. The Manchu faced him, standing stiffly.

"This ship's motors are warm!" Chevski said sharply.

"Yes, Comrade," Shan Bao said politely. "The Colonel Granatman said to keep it warm, he might wish to use it for a flight."

"A flight?" Chevski said. He looked puzzled. From the shadows, Turk could hear his heart pounding as he sensed what was coming. "What flight?"

"Along the coast," the Manchu said simply. "He said he might want to fly along the coast."

Chevski leaned forward tensely.

"The *coast*? Granatman said that?" He stared at Shan Bao. "If you're lyin'—" He wheeled and strode from the hangar. As he stepped past Turk, his breath was coming hard, and his eyes were dilated.

The instant the door closed, Shan Bao's eyes turned to Turk.

"We must work fast, comrade. It was a lie."

Madden stepped out.

"A shrewd lie. He knows something, that one." Turk hesitated, then he looked at the Manchu. "You don't miss much. Have you seen a man with a Berdianka? You know, one of those old model rifles. You know, with a *soshki*? One of those wooden props to hold up the barrel?"

"I know," Shan Bao nodded. "There was one. A man named Batoul, a half-breed, has one. He meets frequently with Comrade Chevski in the woods. He threw it away this day. Now he has a new rifle."

"So," Turk smiled. "The ship is warmed up?"

Shan Bao nodded.

"I have started it every hour since you were taken and have run the motor for fifteen minutes. I thought you might need it. Did you have to kill many men getting away?"

"Not one." Turk smiled. "I'm getting in. When I give the word, start the motor that opens the doors. I'll be going out."

Shan Bao nodded.

"You did not kill even one? It is bad. But leave the door open in the cabin. I shall go with you. I was more fortunate—I killed one."

Turk sprang into the Grumman. The motors roared into life. Killed one? Who? He waved his hand, and the doors started to move, then the Manchu left the motors running and dashed over. He crawled into the plane as it started to move. From outside there was a startled shout, then the plane was running down the icy runway. A shot, but the Grumman was beginning to lift. Another shot. Yells, they were in the air.

He banked the amphibian in a tight circle and headed for the mountains. They'd get him, but first he'd lead them to the coast, he'd let them see for themselves that something was wrong.

In the east, the skies grew gray with dawn. The short night was passing. Below him the first ridges of the mountains slid past, dark furrows in a field of snow.

Shan Bao was at his shoulder. Two planes showed against the sky where he pointed. Turk nodded. Two—one was bad enough when it was a fast pursuit job. One was far ahead of the other.

Madden's eyes picked out the gray of the sea, then he turned the plane north along the coast to the mouth of the Nahtohu. That was the place—and that long reeflike curving finger. That was it.

Ahead of him a dark plane shot up from the forest and climbed in tight spirals, reaching for altitude. Turk's jaws set. That was the plane that got Lutvin. He fired a trial burst from his guns and pulled back on the stick. The two planes rose together. Then the pursuit ship shot at him, guns blazing.

Turk's face was calm, but hard. He banked steeply, swinging the ship around the oncoming plane, opening fire with all his guns.

Suddenly the gray light of dawn was aflame with blasting guns as the two ships spun and spiraled in desperate combat. Teeth clenched, Turk spun the amphibian through a haze of maneuvers, side-slipping, diving, and squirming from position to position, his eight guns ripping the night apart with streaks of blasting fire. Tracers streamed by his nose, then ugly holes sprang into a wing, then he was out of range, and the streaking black ship was coming around at him again.

In desperation, Turk saw he had no chance. No man in an amphibian had a chance against a pursuit job unless the breaks were with him. Like an avenging fury, the black ship darted in and around him. Only Turk's great flying skill, his uncanny judgment of distance, and his knowledge of his ship enabled him to stay in the fight.

Suddenly, he saw the other two planes closing in. It was now or never. He spun the ship over in a half-roll, then shoved the stick all the way forward and went screaming for earth with the black ship hot on his tail. Fiery streams of tracer shot by him. His plane shot down faster and faster.

The black, ugly ridges of the mountains swept up at him. Off to one side he saw the black shoulder of a peak he remembered, saw the heavy circle of cloud around it and knew this was his chance. He pulled the Grumman out of the power-dive so quickly he expected her wings to tear loose, but she came out of it and lifted to an even keel.

Then, straight into that curtain of cloud around the mountain he went streaking, the black pursuit ship hot on his tail. He felt the ship wobble, saw his compass splash into splinters of glass as a bullet struck, then the white mist of the cloud was around him, and he pulled back on the stick. The Grumman shot up, and even as it zoomed, Turk saw the black, glistening shoulder of icy black mountain sweep below him. He had missed it by a fraction of an inch.

Below him as he glanced down he saw the streaking pursuit ship break through the cloud, saw the pilot grab frantically at his stick. Then the ship crashed full tilt into the mountain at three hundred miles an hour, blossomed into flame and fell, tangled, burning wreckage into the canyon below.

The Grumman lifted toward the sky, and Turk Madden's eyes swept the horizon. Off to the south, not a half mile away, the two Russian ships were tangled in a desperate dogfight.

Opening the Grumman up, he roared down on them at full tilt. Shan Bao crouched in his seat, the straps tight about his body, his face stiff and cold. In his hands he clutched a Thompson machine gun. The nearer ship he recognized instantly. It was the specially built Havoc flown by Arseniev. The other—

The pilot of the strange ship sighted him, and, making a half roll, started for him. Madden banked the Grumman as though to escape, saw tracer streak by. Then, behind him, he heard an angry chatter. He made an Immelmann turn and swept back. The pursuit ship was falling in a sheet of flame, headed for the small bay at the mouth of the Nahtohu. The other ship swung alongside, and Turk saw Arseniev raise his clasped hands.

Shan Bao was smiling, cradling the Thompson in his arms like a baby.

"He thought he had us," he yelled. "Didn't know you had a behind gunner."

"A rear gunner, Shan," Turk said, grinning.

Hours later, the Grumman landed easily in the mouth of the Nahtohu.

"See?" Turk said, pointing. "A breakwater, and back there a stone pier, a perfect place for landing heavy armaments. It was ideal, a prepared bridgehead for invasion."

Arseniev nodded.

"Lutvin, he was a good man, but I wonder how he guessed?"

"As I did, I think," Turk told him. He sensed a difference in the coast line, a change. The chart showed no reef there, yet the breakwater was made to look like a reef. As it was, it would give the Japanese a secure anchorage, and a place to land tanks, trucks, and heavy artillery, land them securely."

"That Chevski," Arseniev said. "I knew there was something wrong, but I did not suspect him until he ran for a plane when you took off. But Granatman found the photographs in his belongings, and a code book. He was too sure of himself, that one. His mother, we found, was a Japanese."

Turk nodded.

"Lutvin suspected him, I think."

Arseniev shrugged.

"No doubt. But how could Chevski communicate with the Japanese who flew the guarding pursuit ship? How could he communicate with Japan?"

Shan Bao cleared his throat.

"That, I think I can say," he said softly. "There was a man, named Batoul. A man who wore *unty*, the native moccasins, and one with thong wrappings about the foot. He came and went frequently from the airport."

"Was?" Arseniev looked sharply at the Manchu. "He got away?"

"But no, comrade," Shan Bao protested gently. "He had a queer gun, this man. An old-fashioned gun, a Berdianka with a *soshkin*. I, who am a collector of guns, wished this one above all. So you will forgive me, comrades? The man came prowling

about this ship in the night. He"—Shan Bao coughed apologet-
ically—"he suffered an accident, comrades. But I shall care
well for his gun, an old Berdianka, with a *soshkin*. Nowhere
else but in Siberia, comrades, would you find such a gun!"